LUIS RAFAEL SÁNCHEZ, born in Puerto
Rico in 1936, is a professor of literature at the
University of Puerto Rico. A well-known
playwright, he has also written short stories
and essays. MACHO CAMACHO'S BEAT is
his first novel.

MACHO CAMACHO'S BEAT

LUIS RAFAEL SÁNCHEZ

Translated from the Spanish by
GREGORY RABASSA

A BARD BOOK/PUBLISHED BY AVON BOOKS

Originally published in Puerto Rico as *La Guaracha del Macho Camacho* by Ediciones de la Flor, S.R.L., Argentina

AVON BOOKS
A division of
The Hearst Corporation
959 Eighth Avenue
New York, New York 10019

The Pantheon Books edition contains the following Library of
Congress Cataloging in Publication Data:

Sánchez, Luis Rafael.
  Macho Camacho's beat.

  Translation of La guaracha del macho Camacho.
  I. Title.
PZ4.S19268MAC [PQ7440.S235]   863   80-7713

First Bard Printing, February, 1982

OP 10 9 8 7 6 5 4 3 2 1

Life is a phenomenal thing,
frontwards or backwards, however you swing.

To ALMA, JORGE, and ARCADIO,
for the hours shared

Macho Camacho's Beat

Notice

Macho Camacho's Beat tells of the flattering success of Macho Camacho's guaracha *Life Is a Phenomenal Thing*, according to information received from disk jockeys, announcers, and microphoniacs. It also tells of some miserable and splendid ups and downs in the lives of certain supporters and detractors of Macho Camacho's guaracha *Life Is a Phenomenal Thing*. Furthermore, as an appendix to *Macho Camacho's Beat*, transcribed in its entirety is the text of Macho Camacho's guaracha *Life Is a Phenomenal Thing*, so as to afford unsurpassed delight to collectors of all-time musical hits.

IF YOU TURN around now, a cautious turn, a cautious look, you'll see her sitting and waiting, calmness or the shadow of calmness passing through her. She's got a dreamer's face, a wake me up and touch me face, her legs crossed in a cross. You'll see her sitting and waiting on a sofa: her arms open, bracelets on her arms, a small watch on one wrist, rings on her fingers, over her left heel an anklet with a trinket on it, on each leg a knee, on each foot a striking big shoe. A restless body, she has a body of oh cut it out, can you see?, a body that she sits down, lays out, and plops onto a sofa upholstered with a woolen material that's useful for overcoming polar chills but most unreal for any use in these tristes tropiques: the sun carries out an ungodly vendetta here, it stains the skin, prostitutes the blood, roils the senses: here is Puerto Rico, the successive colony of two empires and an island in the Archipelago of the Antilles. Sweaty too, you'll see her waiting sweaty, sweaty and plopped onto a sweaty ploppy sofa, a sweaty ploppy sofa that changes into a bed that changes into a sofa, an elegant member of a transvestite domestic cast that can do everything. The way her can can. If you turn around now, a cautious turn, a cautious look, you'll see her waiting, sweaty, in spite of the shower of a little while ago. Did they hear her showering? Impossible: she was guarachaing. Under the shower, guaracha and woman in a mating of superb agitation: voice unleashed, body bumping bathroom walls, the shower curtain's guaracha whiplash

5

whacks, soaked in trills, faithful to all balling. Body and soul: springboards for a spree.

TURN AFTER TURN, to shoo away the buzzing of the time she has more than enough of today, today Wednesday, today Wednesday afternoon, today Wednesday five post meridiem, she hums Macho Camacho's guaracha and she makes it louder with the striking stomp of a striking big shoe: *life is a phenomenal thing:* the crowning aphorism of the guaracha that's taken over the country, the crowning aphorism or something like that, a guaracha you people have danced to or listened to or bought or asked for on some radioed program, it doesn't matter whether it's sung or hummed. The crowning aphorism or something like that wavers like an Olympian snow swan, she shakes her head with a raunchy rhythm: raunchiness is my thing: cackled by a dozen showy ha-ha teeth. Turn after turn, to shoo away the time that this afternoon is crinkling in her soul like a crepe-paper wreath, she looks over the apartment with eyes fired up with disdain, crushes the underarm shield, gets a cigarette, straightens the hang of a cheap earring that pretends to be coral. I say that the main thing is appearances: she declares with a haughty grimace: you can always count on her: if I fall down nobody picks me up: like they say a heart of cork to float when it thunders, when it rains, or when the wind blows. Turn after turn, scratching because of an itch brought on by impatience, she walks over to a curtain that hides some gaudy windowpanes: the architecture of our time influenced by the art of our time: *The latest hit.* With unnecessary stealth, imposed by The Old Man's mania for secrecy, she lifts up an edge of the curtain. Generously, she regales her eyes with the bustling construction of a condominium. With a shoulder she brushes the curtain aside deliciously: *it's coffee for breakfast and bread that you eat,* swaying from top to bottom, won over by the delights propounded in Macho Camacho's guaracha, ignorant of the peace and quiet of waiting. It's all waiting, it's all looking at her watch a hundred times, it's all seeing the sun grow soft, it's all waiting, it's all sitting and standing and sweaty and showered: The Old Man's late this afternoon. The Old Man's later than ever. The Old Man's later than never. The Old Man's later than the last time he was late: declarative sentences projected onto the panoramic screen of her vexation, The Old Man's lateness has shaped her vexed reflections, standing by the curtain.

I DON'T DIG his trick of coming late. Of coming when the idea comes to him from wherever it comes. Passing through where the sun doesn't shine on the arrangement we've arranged: contracted for late afternoon and sunset sessions, island Belle de Jour. She specified that she couldn't make it in the early evening or into the night, at seven o'clock I turn into a pumpkin: a household whore version of Cinderella. Nor could The Old Man make it in the early evening or into the night: the responsibilities connected with my roles as a public and a private man, slavery dictated by the hourglass of duty. No, sir, I don't dig his trick of coming late, no, no, no: an unpleasant aftertaste in the superego of a time from days gone by: *María Cristina wants to govern me.* After we do what we do, laboris fornicatio, he climbs into his car of cars and nice as you please he goes off in his car of cars: the superlative refers to a Mercedes-Benz with all the grillwork and novelties of the moment,

7

with the outstanding additive of a front seat that tilts back until it's on the same level as the back seat: an emergency bed for emergency coitus: a kind of unresisted caress for my nature as a ladies' man: The Old Man states. And nice as you please he goes off in his big car after unloading the usual freakeries, freakeries that I listen to as if I cared but which I don't give a damn about: because what is proper always takes precedence: a teaching I drank in from the Napoleonic Code, just imagine, sweet dark girl of my native land, that I'm caught by these licentious urges, licensed attorney that I am, everybody imagining me and expecting me to be at the fulfillment of my official duties: all said with the Platonic air of a dutiful official, a stern voice and a masked threat to recite something tacky like *The Bohemian's Toast*. Freaky as he is, flaky as he is. With the same dumb shit as always. With more *s*'s than a slow fart. With more aroma than a jug of spirits of eucalyptus. Since I'm the one who's got to get on the bus and not him. Since I'm the one who's got to put up with the pawing I get on the bus and not him. Since I'm the one who has to get home at all hours and not him. And because I got home late I've missed the Iris Chacón show on television twice already.

SCANDALIZED, HER BREATH gone, overwhelmed by an anxiousness that had a lot of ness about it, the oxygen held back in her lungs: she adores the performer Iris Chacón, she's papered the little house in Martín Peña with covers from *Vea, Teveguía, Avance, Estrellas, Bohemia* where the performer Iris Chacón is the supreme offering of a national eroticism: the envy of tight-twats, the masturbation fantasy of thirteen-year-olds, the wet dream of adult males, the basis for royal roguery. And the two times I missed the Iris Chacón show on television they told me that Iris Chacón had been out of this world, had run away with it, had been too much. And the two times I missed the Iris Chacón show on television they told me that they'd put the camera on Iris Chacón's belly and the woman looked like she was falling apart from so much wiggling, like she was an electric mixer, like she was an electric mixer with an attack of nerves. The fact is that Iris Chacón has got lots of salsa between skin and flesh: a totalizing and key appendage so that the oxygen that's gone comes back, so the air lock can be opened. Turn after turn: oh drop it, let him come when he has to come or let him take his problem to some other tenement and if he wants to take his problem to some other tenement then he can screw himself on wheels: to clarify things, Clara and me. The Old Man passes me pesos but people who pass me pesos are people I want to pass me pesos. As if I didn't, psst. As if they didn't, psst. As if a person didn't, psst. I've got fucking to spare. I've got more than enough types who want to grab me as soon as I hit the street. I've got enough studs who want to mount me for myself and five other women: the lifts I'm offered, if I set out accepting lifts I wouldn't know what it was like to ride the bus for the rest of my days. The fact is I'm not for pickups, psst. The men who follow me, right behind like dragonflies, real clean-cut types, a whole flock of sweet babies. Proof that if I drop The Old Man I can grab whatever I want. Proof that my thing is making men wild. Proof that my thing is what it is. Proof that my thing is sugar cane. Proof that I'm as good as La India. Proof that I'm not good, that I'm better than good.

PROOFS IN CAPITAL letters that her attractions are highly valued in the tight darkness of trouser flies. She was telling the truth, of course, and as truth it should be endorsed, proclaimed: Sansón, a stumpy little man from El Relincho, wants to put her in charge of the back room of a candy store that conceals two beds for faggotry; Sansón has commercial relations with closeted and uncloseted fairies because Sansón is a bugger who circulates through the urinals of the Parque Muñoz Rivera and the Parque de la Convalecencia; a numbers banker at Stop Fifteen named Deogracias Castro offers her the earnings of twenty books and the loan of a hair-drier pawned with him by a lady souse; a Vietnam veteran with his insides shot up, Pijuán Gómez, guarantees her half of his pension as a schizoid soldier, besides naming her sole heiress of his possessions in case I shit on my mother and kick the bucket before you do; The Turk, a conga drummer from Villa Cañona, swears that he'll get her a dance act at the Lorraine movie theater, an act that she would do under the stage name of The Lobster Lady: you've got all your food in the rear. A price solicited by big-spending johns for the diligent bestowal of said favors: fire her up, give her their bullwhip, hit her with the rod Pancuco lost: offers of an aggressive love that she receives without celebration. How high a position she gives herself because it's not a matter of throwing herself away either: Aristotelian in spite of herself: virtue is the midpoint between two extremes: I don't smile any more than is called for. Psst.

GENEROUS IS SHE and as such regales the busy construction of a condominium with her eyes; the eyes, swinging from one to another like bad acrobats, leap over half a dozen steel drums, inspect the scaffolding that an inspector is inspecting, bump into the concrete kiss and the noise, flutter about the fleshy pole a mason pisses with as she shouts to them: up, up, shouted after having made a mental evaluation of the mason pissing at five o'clock: a peeping mom, bountiful in her gaze. Inevitably the sudden words of the guaracha: *the trumpet breaking up the ball*, the trumpets plow the furrows, the trumpets speak of clandestine rites, the trumpets speak of mounted bodies, the trumpets speak of the hot encounter of one skin with another, the trumpets speak of slow, spasmodic undulations: the trio of trumpeting trumpets. Turn after turn, she sits down to wait sitting down, to wait sweaty on the sweaty sofa, vox populi has it that African fires scorch the isle of Puerto Rico, to wait in perspiration: because the light has gone, because the light goes every afternoon, because the afternoon doesn't work, because the air-conditioning doesn't work, because the country doesn't work; she'd heard it just like that when she was taking the bus to the fortunate apartment. And it wasn't said by a hippie with pollen-messy hair and the languid look of an acid-pothead Christ. It was said by a proper man: the country doesn't work, the country doesn't work, the country doesn't work: repeated to the point of provocation, repeated like the zéjel at the end of a guaracha: facing a red light that was black because the traffic signal wasn't working, the proper man indignant, his stomach contracted with indignation, his mandibles rigid: the country doesn't work. The passengers signed up in two opposing parties: one a minority of timid people in agreement and the other a vociferous majority who proceeded to intone with a verve reserved for national anthems Macho Camacho's irrepressible guaracha *Life Is a Phenomenal Thing*, the deeper tones provided by the driver: wiry and skinny, a wild guarachomaniac; the bus afire with the shrieks and roars of the majority party, the bus afire with the torches of happiness held high by the passengers of the vociferous majority party: happy because with the neat swipe of a guaracha they had crushed the attempt at dissidence, the bus afire with hand-clapping and the figures of those who broke out into dancing and prancing in the narrow aisle, on top of the seats, on top of the wheel, the driver's back transformed into a conga drum by a refrigerator repairman who showed himself to be a musical arranger. She thinks what she thought: a spree is for me and joined in with the guarachaing: she guarachaed until her body told her: baby, sit down. But she paid no attention and gave her ass over to the beat of Macho Camacho's guaracha, the beat of Macho Camacho's guaracha made mincemeat of her ass, a big ass hers. Her legs crossed in a cross, she uncrosses her legs, huffs and rehuffs and fans away sweat, today Wednesday, today Wednesday afternoon, today Wednesday five post meridiem.

SHE TIGHTENS UP her mouth because she's got a cocacolated belch, incredibly strong, which she gulps down in the midst of the guaracha's awakening sounds. The pop in the soda pop, acidity, chronic flatulence, rum, constipation, the bowl of cottage cheese she'd put away at one sitting, the ghostly return of the black coffee, the kicking her spleen had got from the morning beer, the anxiousness that cuts me in two when I have to wait? She reasons like a pair of dice, like a little grain of Red Seal rice: months it's been since I've physicked or magnesiaed myself, centuries since I drank any genipap juice, genipap juice washes the kidneys. The placement of the belch is perfect: between the shrill of the trumpets and the downpour of beats that explode on the bongó, a guttural bluster or an improvised atonal descent that His Holiness Louis

Armstrong would applaud with a musicous encyclical endorsed with feverish sounds. The belch having vaporized, the flatness of her nose recovers its shape, is she Chinese, Japanese, Korean?: more than one person has thought, her face as flattened out as the lid of a cookie tin: a washed-face mulatto girl is what she is.

A WELL-AIMED indifference stuns her, she's got a face that's far away, look at her, as if she had something else in her veins, what, a different liquid substance. Is what's fucking her up liquid? Can what's fucking her up be transmuted into plasma? Look at her now that she's not looking, back without anger from that mess of being a lover under heavy wraps, this hurtful combat and the other thing. As if indifference were the way out, a hundred-proof coldness were the way out, coldness only apparent? Did she learn the sweet charm of pretense from the mannerisms that reverberate out of the magnificent snake-long soap opera *The Son of Ángela María* that had turned the island's heart to honey?: the whole country in suspense over the vicissitudes of Marisela and Jorge Boscán. Did she indeed learn that life is a phenomenal thing from Macho Camacho's guaracha?, a slogan that sweeps everything along, inciting to permanent partying, an evangelical ode to happy happenstance: we've happened onto the Bible. There are things that never become known, the mystery of the world is a world of mystery: a quotable quote. What is well known is that for her everything is plink, it's well known from her own mouth. Listen to her: for me everything is plink. Listen to this other one: everything slips away from me. Lend an ear to what you hear: I can wiggle through anything. And, right away, she shrugs her shoulders, twists her mouth, snorts through her nose, shuts off her eyes: clichés turned serious by the commonality *I don't give a whore's hard turd for anything:* her Lord's Prayer. Don't look at her now because she's looking now.

AND, LADIES AND gentlemen, friends, because the distinguished public says so and the distinguished public is the one who says so and I say that what it says gives cause for fear, it continues as the first and undeniable favorite of the distinguished public through the number one hit parade of Antillean radio, transmitted by the number one radio station or the number one wireless station of the Antillean quadrant, with a superantenna mounted on the supersummit of the supercountry, it continues, I repeat for the benefit of the radio audience who

SENATOR VICENTE REINOSA—Vince is a prince and easy to convince—is tied up, held up, caught up. He says: I'll come late. I'll come late: says he twice. Once, twice, worse, a curse, and he doesn't tear out a couple of hairs because he only has a couple of hairs, skillfully arranged and held in place with lacquered naturalness by the stylist recommendation of a barber become one. Looked at with crass objectivity, the man isn't so bad-looking, but he isn't so good-looking either. Although looking neither bad nor good is a way of looking like anybody. Since you people have him before you, all handsome Glostora ad, all the appreciable gallantry of a gallant who crosses the threshold of Clubman, you decide whether he looks good or bad or whether he doesn't look either good or bad. Senator Vicente Reinosa—Vince is a prince with a conscience to evince—is tied up, held up, caught up in a traffic jam as phenomenal as life, Made in Puerto Rico, the tie-up is an active sample of the Latin American capacity for obstruction, a criminal tie-up, one might say modeled after Julio Cortázar's story *The Southern Thruway:* tobesure, tobesure, life does copy literature. Senator Vicente Reinosa—Vince is a prince and his goodness doesn't wince—snacks on some succulent slices of cuticle, refuses bile entry to his buccal cavity, loosens the necktie that is guillotining him: guillotined by Oscar de la Renta. His cup of desperation drained to the last drop and his thermos of distress run dry, with histrionics outlawed at the Old Vic and the thick and ringing tones worthy of a small-town poetry-declaimer, he recites:

FUCK IT UP, fuck it down, fuck it all around: I won't say I'll come late so as not to sin through inexact usage of the mother tongue. But, I say very late; lateness will impose haste on the fornication. And hasty fornication is a procedure that for my part has never been to my liking. And my established credentials as a tempestuous lover and my widespread fame as a meticulous wooer: a sort of fucking superstar, will suffer the consequences of a haste for which I'm not responsible. Situations like the one I'm going through and enduring now are attacks on the maintenance, propagation, and perpetuation of the continental tradition of the Latin lover. And attacks against the unattainable cult of the genital deeds of Ricardo Montalbán and me, Fernando Lamas and me, Porfirio Rubirosa and me, Carlos Gardel and me, Jorge Negrete and me, Mauricio Garcés and me, Braulio Castillo and me, Daniel Lugo and me: the ascending emotion of an ascending kite. History will judge why he said what he said, history will study the context in which he said what he said: I shit on the jack of clubs. History will decide why he said what he said with

A BOOMING VOICE that Senator Vicente Reinosa— Vince is a prince for the poor long since—thinks is a modulated boom so that it blends with the meteoric force of my meteoric personality: deep breathing in which victorious intolerances swim, an accordionic smile that is always at the sempiternal

18

disposal of corporation presidents and a few vice-presidents too, gifts that merit his elevation to a sainthood of well-known tutelages: a speech for the Lions, a talk for the Rotarians, the darling of industrialists, the bimonthly discourser of the Committee for the Defense of Free Enterprise, the permanent rhapsode of the Catholic Daughters of America, who close their eyes, intoxicated with his prodigious eloquence. He has been Man of the Year two years: the first time when he introduced in the legislature the resolution whereby the messianic presence of American troops in Vietnam was endorsed, the second when he moved and moved along a national campaign for which he coined the slogan *Yankee this is home,* with the aim of offsetting the ungrateful effect of the *Yankee go home* campaign initiated and led by the usual antisocial groups; he was Man of the Year two years and the adopted son of seven towns that in civil wars of venomous fliers and thunderous lampoons claimed the successive anniversaries of his birth for their jurisdictions: with the sworn testimony of seven midwives who guarded in the immeasurable truth of their seven Bibles the evidence of seven little senatorial umbilicals; the first cutting of hair, baptism, losing his baby teeth: in two towns the Municipal Assembly sponsored identical investigations to find the whereabouts of the mouse who did away with the baby teeth of the now famous, illustrious, and eminent man, as he is periodically called in periodicals.

SENATOR VICENTE REINOSA—Vince is a prince and his skill deserves a plinth—looks at his watch, looks at the metallic gleam given off by thousands of hoods corraled together in the sun, he looks at yawns, he looks at grunts, he looks at insults, he looks at a pound of goddammits thrown at the asphalt, he looks at a tune carried along little by little, carried a cappella, carried by an anonymous throat, anonymous and collective, anonymous, collective, and domesticated, a throat that prefers the sedative proposed by the guaracha that has corroded the country, taken over the country: *life is a phenomenal thing.* The tune carried along little by little infiltrates the six bottled-up lines, transforms its little by little into a sour whisper, deafening, whisper and wingding and guff as a national dogma of salvation: the country invaded. For several reasons that are one: rejection of an unbridled galloping ejaculation in favor of a condimented trotting ejaculation, Senator Vicente Reinosa—Vince is a prince and his ideas convince—shits on the Christian deity and holds in low esteem the advice that cowled sisters offered him when he learned about the ineffable pleasures of holy communion: let the sacred form dissolve upon your tongues, abandon ye to the precious sacrament of the Eucharist. This time, forty-five years after, after bending his knees before a dozen images, after depriving himself of eating meat for eternal Fridays of rigorous veto, after citing the lamentations of Job, the confessions of Saint Augustine, the epistles of Saint Paul, after spending nights awake on schoolboy retreats, after being noteworthy for the gift of a Slavic icon to the church where he scrubs off his sins, without misgivings, without atavistic obedience, without ancestral considerations, he shits vilely on the Host. He shits on the Host and he chews it, chewed until he savors its reduction to the food of a ruminant. He also shits, as if in passing, on the blessed chalice and leans on the button of the horn: a long time.

A LONG TIME: the reality round about abolished by closed eyes, the reality round about reinvented by closed eyes:

strong winds that blow and carry off big women, great big women like the Amazons of California: dark, darkies, very dark, vanilla-colored, black as telephones, black as coal; big women, great big women like the Amazons of California, their natural condition of big women, great big women like the Amazons of California adulterated by the furious multiplication of their hairy, cavernous sexes: twenty hairy, cavernous sexes distributed on every body, bursting forth like mushrooms, bursting forth like thistles: indiscriminately; big women, great big women like the Amazons of California who jumble around him, around the hooved satyr, his normal condition of hooved satyr adulterated by the furious multiplication of his hairy, lengthened sex: twenty hairy, lengthened sexes distributed about his body, bursting forth like weeds, bursting forth like lipomas: indiscriminately. The big women, great big women like the Amazons of California begin the seduction of the hooved satyr: like hissing squids, they force the entry of his twenty hairy, lengthened sexes into their hundreds of hairy, cavernous sexes. The numerical disproportion fatigues the hooved satyr, the hooved satyr prepares his flight, to the court-yard of the Corona Brewery. The big women, great big women like the Amazons of California, dark, darkies, very dark, vanilla-colored, black as telephones, black as coal, receive the message sent them by the monitor of their women's intuition and surround him and proceed to decock him: a goodly time at the decocking, a lot of time and a lot of shouting: the reality round about reconquered by a horde of horns.

HE LOOKS AT it again: five to five: the watch sweats in solidarity: a Piaget that flattens the wrist fortified with morning exercitations: Charles Atlas' dynamic tension: his body and his eloquence are whippy. But what's called tied up, held up, caught up is what's with Senator Vicente Reinosa—Vince is a prince and as honest as chintz—because of the jam that's put together every afternoon in the stretch that goes from the Puente de la Constitución to the Avenida Roosevelt along the route of the old slaughterhouse. Sweat that testifies to the sun's vendetta on the here: the here is this unprotected concrete island named Puerto Rico. Sweat dried with a handkerchief of punctilious thread. Sweat protected by a parapet of Vetiver de Craven fragrance: elegance is his forte: a month ago his onomastic appellation and figure figured in the hard-fought election of the country's best-dressed men, an outstanding event that produced productions before television cameras and in sabbath supplements. An outstanding event that produced requests from boutique owners and lady editors of women's pages for his opinion about the return to the tastes of the thirties because of the influence of the film *The Godfather:* is there a nostalgic feeling on the horizon?, will men's hats come back?, will the dark swallows come back? Elegance and oratory are his forte: recently an anthological volume of oratorical prose went to press which has *a cataract in green apocalypse, the man of telluric ruddiness* as a note in the extensive and dedicatory prologue by a Minervan exegete, a poetaster and voting member of four academies of the language. Elegance, oratory, and women are his forte: insomniac animal between his legs.

AT FIVE O'CLOCK in the afternoon, at five o'clock sharp in the afternoon, and it's five on all clocks, the stretch that goes from the Puente de la Constitución to the Avenida Roosevelt along the route of the old slaughterhouse is the hell that is so feared or its principal branch office. When it's not the rancid smell of the burst guts of a public-domain mongrel or the fumes created in the municipal dump or the gas escapes in the refineries of Palo Seco: gases that stink like first-class shit, it's the heavy wave of dust, not to mention the quasi-rehearsed vehicular standstill: like a tin Mammoth, belly ripped open, a Sea Land truck, next to it the derrick that gives it artificial respiration, little motorbikes that bounce through the few openings, the Dodge fleet that returns from the docks of Stop Seven, a little Payco bus, hundreds of cars. There isn't a single tree: if there had been, its liquidation would have been plotted immediately. There is, yes, an abundance of heat and many, very many guarachomaniac drivers and passengers, like patients in a contagion, in an epidemic of a virus of assing and swaying and *it's coffee for breakfast and bread that you eat:* the national industry of poking fun.

SENATOR VICENTE REINOSA—Vince is a prince, no accidents, clean rinse—thought to cut down the Avenida Muñoz Rivera and get to the Avenida Roosevelt via the Calle Quisqueya, but he remembered, fuck of all fucks, that at the Roberto Clemente Municipal Coliseum today they are holding the First National Festival of Drum Majorettes with the coveted prize of a trip to the White House to twirl before the Nixonian condescension of Tricia and Julie and that at Hiram Bithorn Stadium today they are celebrating the First National Festival of Blood-Sausage Gobblers with the first prize adjudicated by the university chair of Domestic Sausage Science and that at the Plaza Las Américas today they are celebrating the First National Festival of Acolytes with a grand prize of kissing the Cardinal's hand and consolation prizes of homilies engraved on burnished sea shells. And the congregation of participants, family members, and looters was calculated in figures of the thousands by the police prophetic services. And the police prophetic services predicted transitory difficulties in transit although they would be permanent between three and six o'clock. And it's five o'clock. No way, the escape has escaped him, and now he'll have to suck on the traffic jam and the heat: uf, uf, uf: an interjection that denotes a hot heat, learned in his secret readings of the comic books with

TILLIE AND MAC. A string of annoyances: first the heat, from the heat the sweat, the traffic jam, the foreseen gossip from his wife's lips, his wife nourished on asspirin tablets, the wild bolero the new lady Senator presented everybody with when she wanted to sing in the rotunda because she stated that her thing was to sing; the logrolling of the Senator from his party who with bashful trills, at the last minute, when he was going down the steps of the august Capitol with sex-driven haste, solicited his cosponsorship of a bill to create a hall of honor for the fathers of the Puerto Rican motherland: Washington, Lincoln, Jefferson, and other titans, with full-length gusts of. Excuse the unwarranted and confused interruption, did I hear full-length busts?, he had heard full-length busts. Vincentian thought teletypes: stupid and proud of it. Full-length busts of Washington, Lincoln, Jefferson, and other founding titans of the Puerto Rican motherland, so that our children and our children's children can discover in the majesty of the clobbered stone. Excuse the unwarranted and confused interruption, but did I hear clobbered stone?, he had heard clobbered stone. Vincentian thought teletypes: unsalvageable savage. Discover in the majesty of the clobbered stone the repository of our history. Clasp that closes the string of annoyances: a delay in the yearned-for meeting with the mistress of the moment. Ah, ah, ah, with his neatly hidden love affairs and mistresses he could form a stable: how many fillies: puffing up his cheeks like the fabled frog. Vanity, bragging, a wild hustle and bustle, a me yes and what's the matter adorn the word mistress.

HAVE JUST BEGUN to hear my end-all Popular Disco, which is broadcast from Mondays to Sundays from twelve noon to twelve midnight by the number one radio station and number one wireless station of the Antillean quadrant, continuing in first place and in the indispensable favor of the distinguished audience, after eight weeks of absolute sovereignty, absolute rule, absolute empire, is that slippery and peppery, purgative and instructive, prophylactic and didactic, scatological and eschatological guaracha of Macho Camacho, *Life Is a Phenomenal Thing.*

WITH HER NAILS lacquered by Virginale, a love-trap created by nature, with the coolness and purity of a virgin forest, shades light as the clouds, Graciela Alcántara y López de Montefrío opens her purse: a charming bag of snow-white kidskin charged at Sears, very delicate, very elegant, very expensive, and absolutely necessary for occasions in which a certain careful carelessness becomes pertinent; emblazoned thus by the gods of dernier cri rags: the ostentation of nonostentation: the very casual look: glowing as if she weren't glowing from her glow, wearing with perfect imperfection the little number chosen without choosing, gloria aeterna of grandes dames who moan the litany of what do I have to wear: smothered in labyrinths of chiffon, Italian silk prints, and couturier extravagances from Givenchy, Halston, and Balmain, not to mention Martin, Carlota Alfaro, and Mojena. Graciela Alcántara y López de Montefrío draws from her charming bag of snow-white kidskin: very delicate, very elegant, very expensive, the fine gold vanity charged at Penney's: a border of hyacinth ending in a bow. A gentle snap and open vanity. First a flattering smile—flattering?—for the receptionist who is reading the thirtieth edition of the novel *Her Husband's Other Woman,* by Corín Tellado, a reading done to a reverberating musical background of Macho Camacho's guaracha *Life Is a Phenomenal Thing.* Footnote without the foot: the receptionist will function as a nurse if things get too hot: and things get too hot when one of the clients or one of the patients resists the comedy of manners and morals, of pleased to meet you, the hand-kissing, the pipe-dream of all quiet on the western front, of Jane Fonda in *Klute:* coolness and analysis.

GRACIELA ALCÁNTARA Y López de Montefrío's cheeks flood the little vanity mirror. Mirror, mirror on the wall: she woos it, she flatters it, she wants to make it her little friend, out of the corner of her eye she scrutinizes the facial zone where capillary vessels are blue: fantasist, escapist, Graciela Alcántara y López de Montefrío sustains a delicate balance between her present age and one lost, invoked by the divine humectants of Helena Rubenstein, a delicate balance that dies in successive spacious salons where the profuse weeping of the lamps has improvised a poetry of illuminated days: a cotillion of debutantes at the Casa de España: a ghetto of peninsular amenities and creole wonders: every surname written has dreams of a crown of splendor shaped by the number of head of cattle, the number of acres under cultivation, the number of acres of grazing land, the number of bank loans, the number of mortgages held, the number of creditors consigned, the number of servile acts secured: there are second sons: beaker-wielders in pharmacies founded long before Americans ate their soup with a big spoon, wholesalers who couldn't get rid of a smell of onion and garlic that couldn't be covered up by their tuxedos, nephews-in-law of the gentleman who has a mill in Tarragona, distant cousins of the gentleman who has his

Galician pazo in Villa de Arosa; a cotillion of debutantes in the Casa de España: a ghetto of peninsular amenities and creole wonders.

THE DÉBUT IN society of Graciela Alcántara y López de Montefrío, one of fifteen cocooned creatures alembicated in the bosom of distinction: the introit of the Andalusian herald who, year after year, with a fanfare of feathers, frilled shirt, and knee breeches presents the cocooned creatures alembicated in the bosom of distinction, the introit of the Andalusian herald once he has struck the floor three times with his staff; a staff of authority in medieval towns. The locution of the Andalusian herald: the fifteen cocoons will embroider upon it with the charm of their feet and the gracious enchantment of their arms, the palatine elegance of the palatine cotillion: tears of mothers and fathers eternalized in little lachrymal boxes from Battersea, a covey of tulles, a covey of organdies, a covey of piqués, a bouquet of forget-me-nots, a bouquet of hydrangeas, a bouquet of bromeliads: courtliness sketched by the slight nod and the slight walk. The locution of the Andalusian herald: fifteen ephebes favored by frivolous Fortune will alert the miracle of the fifteen cocooned creatures alembicated in the bosom of distinction to give Viennese form to that *Blue Danube* that is impatient on the violin strings: tears of mothers and fathers eternalized in little lachrymal boxes from Fabergé. The locution of the Andalusian herald: the fifteen cocooned creatures alembicated in the bosom of distinction, a promise of roses on a rosy morning, abandon themselves with a decorum fertilized by devoted gardeners to their first night in society, oh congregated cream of the constituted crop, I call for a round of cheers for the pride of Medina, for the flower of Olmedo.

GRACIELA ALCÁNTARA Y López de Montefrío, mother-of-pearl fan, strapless bra, hair that would tempt the publicity man for Barry hair-conditioner, hair organized into two bows from which two cascades of ringlets hung, Graciela Alcántara y López de Montefrío, timid and wary because her ephebe favored by frivolous Fortune squeezed her until he was squeezing air, until he was squeezing her thoughts, searched among the small tables surrounding the dance floor for the stern gaze of her widowed mother, her ephebe favored by frivolous Fortune had squeezed her until he had reduced the circumference of her waist to millimeters and had murmured in her ear franked by Majorca pearls: I put my hand into a small gold coffer and drew out the sweet name of Ciela; I will never forget the offer: which he never forgot until the next dance, a bolero by Sylvia Rexach: *I am the sand the wave has never touched.* Because when Graciela Alcantara y López de Montefrío drew back, resisted the indecent shortcut taken by his arm, the ephebe favored by frivolous Fortune felt that he was being mistreated, ridiculed: a down for his little pride put up on a dais by telephonic demands from little girls taking their first steps in the sport of manhunting: they danced, yes, with a displeasure and annoyance offensive to a first night in society, César Concepción's orchestra with his exclusive vocalist Joe Valle; at home, while going through the process of undoing the bows from which two cascades of ringlets hung, Graciela narrated the incident to her widowed mother with every jot and tittle, the sorrows of having been born a woman: they wept: her widowed mother made her decision: you're going abroad, you're going to Switzerland snowy and pure, you're going far away from the insular vulgarity which it is a Christian duty to flee: sign of the cross. During the weeks that followed the press wagged its tongue about the successful entry into society of Graciela Alcántara y López de Montefrío: the cover of *Alma Latina*, a photographic locket in *Puerto Rico Ilustrado*, the incorporation of the historic event into the chronicles of Miguel Ángel Yumet, Carmen Reyes Padró, and Lady Boix de Buxeda: a coincidence in the epithets that were dusted off: angelic bearer of innocence, fresh as a child bride, bubbling with joy, the bearing of an Infanta of Spain:

A PAINFUL TRIP through the looking-glass, Graciela Alcántara y López de Montefrío isn't Alice, but she travels through the looking-glass, an intermirroral traveler, in the parturient trees of her parturient imagination there awaits the shadow spread by the sweet bird of youth: bewildered, trembling, weepy, she resists the provocation of the obscene bird of night: lewd and demanding: better dead than given over to libidinous parties, dead or bled by the birds that go to die in Peru. Alas and alack for her who had been beautiful! Coming soon on this face: a mask of salt and yogurt, a mask of starch and sandalwood, a mask of spices filtered with a pinch of vanilla scent and saffron. *Rrrriiinnnggg:* what a start, her heart leaps into her mouth but docile after the complaint it goes back to the heart of her insides. The receptionist: Miss, you have to calm those nerves. *Rrrriiinnnggg.* The receptionist lowers the volume of the transistor. The silence, compact as a hippopotamus, erases *a phenomenal thing*. *Rrrriiinnnggg*, third *rrriiinnnggg*, three are the rings awaited before lifting up the telephonic apparatus and answering: advice offered in the column by Ann Landers inserted into little manuals of secretarial efficiency and ratified by the little course of Swiss refinement.

HELLO, HELLO, PEPSI'S mellow: colonized ingenuity. Office of the Psychic and Psychosomatic Practice of Dr. Severo Severino . . . Being sorry to tell you that your request is quite impossible . . . Quite impossible during the present week and during the weeks that will be present in coming weeks . . . A great many depressed ladies . . . I said the lady is so depressed that she's swimming in it . . . I repeat that the depressed lady is too much . . . I say that you could make a dragnet of all the depressed ladies in San Juan . . . Send her to Disneyland . . . A meeting with Pluto might give her back the desire to live . . . Buy her some chocolate ice cream . . . Dr. Severo Severino will get back to you.

BY EMINENT DOMAIN Macho Camacho's guaracha returns, a transistor that spits out deliriums of phenomenal life. Mirror, mirror on the wall, she gives a little piece of candy to the little mirror so it will be her little friend, she opens her eyes wide, winks long, winks slowly, like a neurotic doll, like a doll with a soft backside, like a doll with a short spring, like a doll with a fragile, irritated eye, like a decunted doll. Silent anguish, the I don't know what, the I do know what, the it isn't nausea but it's got the face of nausea, she converses with the anguish that seeks her along the temples: a bastion of folds or a nest of vipers. Coming soon on this face: a mask of egg and camphor, a mask of egg yolk and dew, a mask of egg white and mint juice. Mirror, mirror on the wall: Graciela investigates the spot hidden by the stroke of Balcony Amber, a beeswax crayon charged at Chez Bamboo, the little mirror absorbs a clump of adolescent wrinkles for which Graciela beseeches the charity of modesty; any morning now, taking the rhythm of the fortyish prose, the bundle of wrinkles will take over Graciela's skin and devastate it, it is written in the book of life and subtly announced in the marks left by crows' feet. This evening on this face: a mask of ripe banana and alligator pear with a drop of mint extract, Graciela Alcántara y López de Montefrío looks at the little watch that hangs over her breast like a locket, with a lyrical sigh she attempts a snort of surfeit. A noisy snap and close vanity. Urgent message: the vanity closed or the vanity remained closed at five o'clock in the afternoon, Wednesday afternoon today.

CLOSE VANITY OF most ladylike lady annoyed by the insidious lilt of that guarachose music that to her was like a vote of confidence in the low-class vulgarity that like an endless lightning flash sweeps the island of Puerto Rico: tropical abode of the trashy, springboard of the sassy, closed paradise of depravity. A vocal outburst: but *life is a nice chubby chick.* Fine lady refined in a Swiss refinement school where her widowed mother sent her, her widowed mother tormented by the noisy insular vulgarity which it was, is, and will be a Christian duty to flee; sign of the cross, disgusted, outraged because the moral lightning rod didn't work, evidenced by the consent and back-

ing of a life bound by the book-covers of decency: there is a
crop of women who call men by the familiar form, who are
born for evil or evil born.

LITTLE FISH FISHED out of the river roiled by Gracie-
lan thought: how beautiful is beauty. Graciela feels a feeling:
Switzerland snowy and pure, her widowed mother, her engage-
ment to the fine and refined, gentleman and gentlemanly first-
class boy: interminable sessions of interminable rocking in the
interminable chairs on the interminable balcony of the interminable ancestral home on the interminable Calle Loíza under
the interminable look of the interminable widow who was her
interminable mother; marriage to the fine and refined, gentleman and gentlemanly first-class boy: the church a garden of
gillyflowers and lilies of the valley and noble scents in Italian
vases greened by wild ferns and a sprig of silver fir; a goodly
number of invited guests, people slipping in, church biddies
left over from rosary and onlookers who abandoned for a while
the cardboard squares of the bingo being played at the parish
house; a flapping and pecking of the Ave Maria intoned diva
style by a superstar from the Grand Opera of Curaçao, a
strutting coloratura who filled the pews of the church with
little cards of boastful introduction and Aldine lettering: *Mimi
Ledoux. Étoile of the Grand Opera of Curaçao. Has own wardrobe.* And, turmoil of turmoils: delirious applause when
Graciela Alcántara y López de Montefrío, most beautiful in her
bridal outfit in which the trim of camellias stood out, solemn
and trembling, made her appearance at the beginning of the
nave on the arm of her only uncle, her lame only uncle. At that
precise moment, a ballbreaker broke loose. The priest, a wrath-
ful Basque from Bilbao, waved the hyssop while his eyes of a

little Nazi owl threw off darts of condemnation; while his bronchitic piccolo voice shouted: in the house of God expressions of worldly enthusiasm are not permitted, a defect of the Pharisees, cursed for time immemorial are those who committed the sin of applause, zero glory for those who clapped their hands. Most ugly piccolo voice, the candles shaken by the breeze aroused by the applause. Graciela remembered pale as the girl from Guatemala, pale as the motionless beloved, beautifully quiet before the turbulence of the acclamations and cheers and the unusual admiration of the acolytes, two sensational prospects for sons of bitches who garbled the response and instead of saying amen said oh man, oh man. Mimi Ledoux, étoile of the Grand Opera of Curaçao, crammed into the projecting choir loft, became enthusiastic with the signs of enthusiasm that she supposed had their origin in her stupendous, grand, unequaled interpretation of the Ave Maria and thought it prudent and mandatory to add a small number of great personal luster in accord with the enthusiasm that had its origin in her stupendous, grand, unequaled interpretation of the Ave Maria: fiery, emulating Tebaldi and Callas, she gave out with the Habanera from *Carmen*, embellished with flamenco trappings like *olé*, the lifting of her skirt, and heel-stamping that put the weakness of the overhanging loft to the test and launched onto the altar the claws and hooves of the fearsome dragon who had been vanquished in his day by that certain George, thereupon made saintly, shortened to saint, dragon and saint who, in hardened plaster, adorned the access to the loft.

AND, LIKE A persistent rainfall, like a foolish little fish that falls time after time into the net of the memory of her honeymoon in Guajataca: motionless visions like confiscated postcards: protected by the chasteness of a camisole of monkish cut and austere lace that, listen to me Ciela, you won't take off even to do the brazen copulative act, what's that Mama?, a frightened banner strung from eye to eye, that's the carnal penetration of his privy part into yours.

AND IT IS not a question, ladies and gentlemen, friends, of a foolish little number that fills the repertory of a musical group like I mean the Afro Babies, the Latin Provocatives, the Top of the Top, the Monster Feeling, the Creole Feeling. I mean that it's not a question of a ditty or some sugary rubbish to sweeten the cheap taste of long-haired types.

"IT'S GOOD FOR him, the sun bath is," The Mother said: she was shaving her legs and putting little saliva stars on the cuts: a dull blade. Like an erratic bat, harried by crude clouds, it flew through the alley and flew through the courtyard and flew over the balcony and flew over the house from end to end, the ritornello of proclaimed morality: *life is a phenomenal thing.* The Mother saddled the ritornello of proclaimed morality with a stentorian swaying and fenced in her eyes in order to fabricate in a trick worthy of the greatest admiration, with backdrops and curtains of her own invention, the stage where her favorite artist had her triumph: the crest of her dream was occupied, as if by a Ceres embellished with branches full of round tomatoes, heads of lettuce, watercress, and slices of alligator pear, by the polychrome, polyfaceted, polyphonic, polyform, polypetaled, polyvalent body of the artist Iris Chacón.

THE MOTHER WANTED to sing little chocolate-candy tunes like Iris Chacón. The Mother wanted to dance like Iris Chacón and gain continental fame with her anarchic buttockry. The Mother wanted to be transformed into another Iris Chacón and lose herself and find herself in the seismic curves

41

that have their starting point at the waist. The Mother wanted to BE Iris Chacón and let her hair down in public like a feverish tigress of the kind announcers call temperamental: squinting with a penetrating look, a low neckline that is offered but never given, mouth half-open. Once transformed into the artist Iris Chacón or made into the artist Iris Chacón or re-treaded as the artist Iris Chacón, she would proceed to indulge men's desires amidst the dazzling long locks, long locks on vacation from the face and its boundaries. Resigned to the meanness of not being who she wanted to be, disposed to accept only a hair from the wolf, The Mother swore that one of these days, after she signed her name, she would add as nice as you please: alias Iris Chacón. The Mother: if I put my mind to it I'd be the end on television: brazen stream of consciousness.

"IT DOES HIM good, the sun bath does," adds The Mother when Doña Chon, our neighbor who art in Martín Peña Channel, asks her why she leaves The Kid abandoned in a sunny spot: the front steps of the Basilica of Saint John Bosco, a small park on the Calle Juan Pablo Duarte: she was spotted in the unconcerned move by The Calf and The N. "The Calf and The N can stick it where it has to be stuck," said The Mother: wide-eyed with her arched mouth brought to putrefaction by toads and serpents. "The Calf can look to the goings-on of that royal daughter she's got and stop digging into garbage cans, the ragpicker," said The Mother. "The N can stop taking Darvon and aspirin, the pill-popper," said The Mother. "What do they mean, abandoned, abandon is what they do with their tongues at full speed, what do they mean

abandoned," said The Mother: fire, smoke, hot coals in her mouth. The Mother lathered her other leg, the safety razor condemned artificial fuzz and exonerated stubble of all blame: "The Old Man goes wild when he fondles hairy legs," said The Mother: a happy bit of news concerning The Old Man's fetishist quirks. Doña Chon, delousing the back of her cat Cuddles, a cat pampered by Doña Chon, gave the word: all those perversions are predicted in the last chapters of the Bible. Doña Chon, delousing the legs of her cat Cuddles, a cat pampered by Doña Chon, gave the word: the one up above will call for an accounting of all those perversions when he comes down. "Sun baths?" said Doña Chon: surprise, disbelief. "It'll get him a good hot fever," said Doña Chon: physician. "It'll get him a bad sunstroke," said Doña Chon: scholar. "In the pretty little hole of his pretty little ass a little growth is going to grow," said Doña Chon, popess, a loving tap on the behind for Cuddles who leaped onto the third shelf of the cupboard. "Sun baths?" asked Doña Chon again. "Don't hand me that," said Doña Chon: face scrawled with skepticism and other philosophical doctrines, ancient and modern.

NO BOOB IS Doña Chon and she wants it to be well known and the knowledge well sown and the word to go out that she's no boob. Doña Chon explains the inference concerning her boobishness from the contusive fact of her contusive fatness. First apocryphal level of Doña Chon in contusive declarations for those of you who think, standing together, that hunger and wanting to eat are the same thing: people go around thinking that us fat people are ninnies. People go around thinking that us fat people are first cousins to Boob

McNutt. Additional fact to keep in mind, independent of what Doña Chon, with her own beak, has told you: Doña Chon is much more than tending toward overweight. Doña Chon is much more than fat. The much more in tercets gives her the thickness of a great big angel bogged down in lard, a great big rebel angel against all buccal abstinence. Confirmed: Doña Chon is no boob, fat people aren't ninnies, fat people aren't first cousins to Boob McNutt. Recognized fact: Doña Chon is as good as gold, as good as golden bread: fermented and cooked wheat dough which she likes to eat.

"THE SUN BURNS away his weakness," said The Mother, dogmatic as a practicing Catholic, dogmatic as a practicing Marxist. "The sun drives out any boobishness," said The Mother, combing her unshaved armpit because "The Old Man likes to fondle my hairy armpit," said The Mother. "The sun like an onion will beg your pardon and do its best to give you a hard-on," said The Mother: conclusively, going to the door, letting Macho Camacho's guaracha take up residence in her waist, twisting and twisty, guarachose and triumphant in imaginary cabarets, surrounded by a focus of lights that made the imprecise lines of her vivid makeup precise, guarachose and triumphant and wrapped in waves of applause: *life is a phenomenal thing,* giving the microphone to the MC. The MC announcing to the audience guarachized by the guaracheries of the queen of the shimmy that the queen of the shimmy will delight them again with the risk of her dangerous curves at the Midnight Show so keep on drinking and doing what I'd do, anchor into some firm flesh and check your oil and wait for the Midnight Show and remember that here and everyplace that

isn't here life is a phenomenal thing, fanfare, Doña Chon helping her take off her spangled belly-band, Doña Chon hanging her spangled bikini on a hook, Doña Chon giving her a drink of Malta Tuborg punch, when in the devil are they going to stop clapping.

"IT WAS A hex they put on me but The Kid caught it," said The Mother, turning around, leaving the door, the razor in her hand. "The Kid was as beautiful as bacon," said The Mother. "The Kid was as handsome as a hambone," said Doña Chon. The Mother and Doña Chon: whiners. "The hex was put on me by the girlfriend of one of my cousins from La Cantera," said The Mother, putting the razor on a cupboard shelf. "A vampire, a lazy bum, a dirty-assed bitch who spread it around that I was a man-stealer," said The Mother. "That same dog has bitten me at least twenty times," said Doña Chon: hieratic. "Me a man-stealer, with fucking to spare," said The Mother. "The pickups I've been offered," said The Mother. "It's just that I'm not for pickups," said The Mother. "Man-stealer, chaser, dollar-a-throw whore she said I was," said The Mother. "And that vampire, that lazy bum, that dirty-assed bitch went straight to Toya Gerena's spirit center and got me a hex with a mammee yam and some goat grease," said The Mother. "And the hex made The Kid hunchbacked for good," said The Mother. "That vampire, that lazy bum, that dirty-assed bitch is called Geña Kresto because before she gets under a man she has to drink a mug of Kresto chocolate," said The Mother. "All that Kresto has done her harm," said Doña Chon, full of prophetic powers. "She's a real savage, that woman," said Doña Chon, analytic. "That woman Geña Kre-

45

sto will have to pay you and pay you well," said Doña Chon, justicialist. "What's done here is paid here," said Doña Chon, talionic. "It wouldn't surprise me if Geña Kresto grew a nest of hairy spiders in her heart," said Doña Chon, apologist for Medean vengeances. "No way, east or west," said The Mother, face scrawled with skepticism and other philosophical doctrines, ancient and modern. "The cousin of mine who knows her dressed and naked says the woman is like a coconut," said The Mother, argumentative. "There are rancid coconuts," said Doña Chon, magnificent and hair-raising, theosophical and anointed with eternal truths, radiant in the manifestation of her chthonic wisdom. With sighs, a touch teary, The Mother and Doña Chon saw:

THE CLOUD OF flies, buzzing Eumenides improvising a furious halo around the large head. The Mother and Doña Chon looked at the drooly face and the drool and the dozing of a fool with the dead lizard in his hand: The Kid chewed the head of the lizard until the tail relaxed its guard, the same tail that, trapped in the throat, had invited vomit. The Mother and Doña Chon looked at the vomit: an archipelago of miseries, bloody islands, necklaces of vomit, vomit like a stew of Chinese broth, thick crystals, Chinese eggdrop soup, a convention of all yellows in the vomit, yellows tattooed by orange juice, yellows relieved by the dirty transparency of the drool, crystals thickened by grains of rice: a vomit as God ordains.

"WHEN HIS PA went to Chicago to pick tomatoes," said The Mother, "because things are bad for people born here," said Doña Chon, "The Kid looked normal," said The Mother. "He was normal at his birthright," said Doña Chon. "It started coming out after he was crawling," said The Mother. "It began with the high fevers he got because his head was growing," said The Mother. "Hollering like he was being killed and he'd roll around against the walls and everything was all bumps and bruises," said The Mother. "The same as when you kill a chicken in the house," said Doña Chon. The Mother and Doña Chon: spoonfuls of Dear Lord. "Then he opened out like a branch with fruit spread all over it," said The Mother. "Like he was the son of Chencha La Gambá, which was a song with a double meaning that Myrta Silva used to sing," said The Mother. "I don't like songs with double meanings," said Doña Chon, her snout turned up.

"MYRTA SILVA USED to sing a lot of songs," said The Mother, "songs she brought back in her baggage from Cuba and Panama, where they say the woman was a queen from the way she had with the maracas and guarachas." "Felipe Rodríguez used to sing a lot of songs," said Doña Chon. "They nicknamed me Heathen Chinky, which was a song Felipe Rodríguez sang, and Mother didn't like them to call me Heathen Chinky because Mother said it sounded like a streetwalker's name," said The Mother. "Felipe Rodríguez married Marta Romero before Marta Romero started singing like a Mexican," said Doña Chon. "Ruth Fernández used to sing a lot of songs," said The Mother. "Ruth Fernández was put across good like singers from outside are and she never wore the same gown twice," said Doña Chon. "Ruth Fernández was a black singer but she was proper," said Doña Chon. "Daniel Santos sang a lot of songs," said Doña Chon, "and Mother used to cry when he sang a number that went *I've come to say goodbye to all the boys because any day I'm off to war,"* said The Mother. "My brother was scrambled in the Korean War," said The Mother: sorrow resting on hoarseness. "Mother turned into a loony and three months later they found her dead from nothing they could find," said The Mother. "She died from wanting to die," said Doña Chon.

"LAST SUNDAY, NO, the one before, I took The Kid to Just Plain Mary's Spirit Temple," said The Mother. "Just Plain Mary has got spirit touches that make up for the punishment of all the mustache hairs that grew out on her when she was twelve years old and started to menstruate," said The Mother. "Just Plain Mary found out about her spirit gifts because she began to spout beautiful things out of her mouth the night she was watching television and the wedding of Just Plain Mary, the real one," said The Mother. "A lot of good dead people are at work for Just Plain Mary," said The Mother. "On the table where she does her work Just Plain Mary has pictures of the late Eva Perón, the late President Kennedy, the late fugitive Correa Cotto," said The Mother. "It's something," said The Mother. "You really can have a good time," said The Mother. "When that guaracha says that life is a phenomenal thing, it's something that's like to eat my brain up," said The Mother. "The day when Iris Chacón sings and dances Macho Camacho's guaracha will be the day to end all days," said The Mother. "The Lord protect us on that day," said Doña Chon, pale in her prophecy of sinister things.

LONGHAIRS AND OTHER kinfolk of the flock. Do you understand me with understanding? Or does the always smiling, always respectable, always listening audience want another exemplary example of what's music music and what's not music music?

BRAKING EVERY MINUTE bothers him, Benny's bother. Braking every minute annoys him, Benny's annoyance. Braking every minute blows him up, Benny's blowup. Braking every minute screwtinizes him, Benny's screwtiny. Braking every minute knocks his balls, Benny's knockers. Braking every minute gores his . . . Benny's goring. Braking every minute knocks, Benny's knockers. This is Benny. This is Benny in chinos. This is Benny in chinos and a polo shirt. This is Benny in chinos, a polo shirt, and tennis shoes, also known as Champions. Benny is stuck in a Ferrari and the Ferrari is stuck in a traffic jam and the jam is a jam in a short side street that flows into a long artery: to save time, to avoid a waste of time, a street that nobody will be taking: mistaken, taken, a side street that everybody is taking to save time, to avoid a waste of time. Foreseen and collective and conscious recognition of the uselessness of protest but: a chorus of horns proceeds, all together, *todos a una,* just like Fuenteovejuna. A volatile roofing of horn-blowing. And, buried by the claxonic dissonance, feeling its way through the uproar, snakes the guarachaing of the three hundred radio sets, a shout of pure salsery: *life is a phenomenal thing.* Indignant but with a guarachile dignity, the autose multitude, the carose multitude, the enwheeled multitude, brakes, guarachas, advances, brakes, guarachas, advances, brakes, guarachas, advances. Benny, chinoed, poloed, championed, is the producer of a sostenuto hornblast, of a sostenuto

51

rage, of a sostenuto mother-curse; the expansion of Benny's mouth is such that

IT LOOKS LIKE a crocodile's. With the crocodile's mouth that looks like Benny's mouth, Benny proceeds to defecate on and on top of the maternal relations of a considerable number of virgins and saints: he had studied in the Theresan Mothers' kindergarten and in the Redemptionist Fathers' high school: by the skirts of both he had suckled the milk of Christian martyrology: bottles of the heretical sect, bottles of the atrocious punishments inflicted upon those who believed correctly, bottles of the exemplariness of faithfulship. Benny defecates, relieves himself, moves his bowels, evacuates, pollutes, befouls, and all other synonyms that proceed from the base, vile, vulgar infinitive *to shit* on the gentilics, appellatives, and patronymics of the honorable people who earned us the choice between heaven and hell. Saint Philigonius, Saint Ausentius, Saint Spiridon, along with their mothers: shat upon, Saint Salome, Saint Tullia, Saint Leocadia, along with their mothers: shat upon.

A FERRULED FERRARI is a frenum to frenzy. A Ferrari is a gift that a Papi Papikins gives to Sonny Sonnikins on the memorable occasion of his eighteenth birthday: once the melopoeia of *Happy Birthday to You* has been intoned by the orpheum of family and famuli, with the exception of Benny's Mami, who always got a splitting headache every time the young sprout had a birthday, into the entranceway burst the car of cars for the dorsal delight and subsequent swoon of

Benny, who had to be revived with handkerchiefs soaked in Superior Setenta alcohol and paternal cajolery and who had to be protected from the speculation that fainting by a male child might arouse in the blunted intelligences of three maidservants: Benny is all man, Benny is a young pigeon with a satyr's hooves, Benny collects harlots, but Benny is also a softy, Benny gets emotional in a crisis, Benny follows the path of Werther and Wally's Edward: a pastoral letter from Papi Papikins to a culinary congregation which he kept happy with winks, flirtation, and pats on the ass, a black-skinned culinary congregation that was fulfilling the task of bringing back to the Beverly Hills mansion everything that had gone with the wind.

WHAT I MEAN is that now I, what I mean is that I now am too big for a party with a cake and candles and loud kisses from Mami and loud kisses from Mami's friends and boxes of handkerchiefs and neckties and cuff links and boxes by Yardley and little bottles of Aqua Velva and dance with little Betty and dance with little Kate and dance with little Mary Ann and dance with little Elizabeth: exhortations concocted in the matrimonial pot of momism through the influence of the populational census that assures us of a critical scarcity of the masculine gender and predicts the hopeless oldmaidhood of thousands of females. What I mean is that my head swims when I hear, hear, hear, Mami, Mami, Mami, tell me, tell me, tell me, low, low, low: tell your friend with the motorcycle that the front wheel of his cycle is hindering the natural tilt of one of the lower branches of my blue hydrangeas: laboriously achieved by the gardener who had to buy grafting soil at Pennock Garden: tell your friend with the long hair not to throw his cigarette butts into the flower beds where my black orchids are growing and tell your friend with the face of a mechanic, the face of a Chicago gangster, the face di tenore not to spit so much in the tubs where my baby's-breath is growing and tell your friend with the dopey look to get off the fragile trunk of my weeping willow: Benny's Mami tempered things with ironic tonal curves, Benny's Mami irritated by the frankness of the hair and the coarse smell: I wonder if behind my back they've organized a state of strike against deodorants and razors; Benny's Mami unaware that the intruders in her molto bello gardeno, as bello as il gardeno degli Finzi-Contini ma non as bello as the garden of forking paths or as extravagant as the garden of delights, are the gay-young-blade offspring of the triumphant castes, the children of louse-ridden reason and unpeeled will. Just between us: alienated and forgotten backtalkers of the collective achievement: believe me. Benny's Mami, who repeats, like the refrain of a guaracha but without charm, without verve, without dash, without fire, without taste or waste of sugar or other sweetnesses:

SAY HELLO, BENNY, smile, Benny. Be sociable, Benny. Stand up straight, Benny. Gentlemen wait for ladies to offer their hand, Benny. Stand up when a young lady speaks to you, Benny. Stand up when a young lady's Mother speaks to you, Benny. Having good manners is a full-time job, Benny. Being refined is a vocation that never ends, Benny. Be fine and refined, a gentleman and gentlemanly, Benny. Follow the example of your father, who is fine and refined, a gentleman and gentlemanly, Benny. And: lacerated by the incomprehension of humankind, a suppliant like her Greek predecessors, a mendicant after elementary respect, a solicitor for faith in the unblemished goodness of her unblemished intentions: Benny, by the health of the Christ of Health, before you give me a heart attack: how do I know what you're going to give me, before they find me dead in the loneliness of these walls: how do I know where they'll find me, before cancer carries me off: how do I know what will carry me off, tell your friends to dance, dance, dance, that people come to parties to dance, dance, dance, that they don't come to parties to talk about cars, that they don't come to parties to talk about car races, that they don't come to parties to talk about the Añasco track, that they don't come to parties to make private jokes. What I mean is that if you ask me what I'd ask for you, I'd ask for a terrific Ferrari, a car of cars: but Papi Papikins, not me, not me.

SO MANY SAINTS shat upon have never been seen before. And Benny's mouth, who would believe it even if he could see it: a latrine or a urinal clogged with the most sordid graffiti. Even the side street with the presumptuous name, Paris, gets its. And the believers in the goddess Mita who are having a party along the Calle París in patrols of three and four get theirs. Ardors freed by civil indignation: or who's ever seen a country without straight streets, or who's ever seen a country without a track for racing cars: his hand worn out from pushing on the rim of the horn so much: the rim of the horn a pentagram on which Benny outlines a supreme combination of notes, his hand worn out from reaching outside the Ferrari to unfurl itself like a flag that makes question marks: question marks that several people babble what the hell's going on up ahead there: but this time Macho Camacho's guaracha seems funereal, heard like a miserere, heard like matins, heard like kyrie eleison: an ecclesiastic salsa played at five o'clock in the afternoon on Wednesday, Wednesday today.

WHAT I MEAN is how did you put over the deal, Papi Papikins. Well, just listen to me, my loving son, let's invite to the hearing those of us who aren't loving sons, I called from the Senate so that the point of origin of the call, that is, the influence popularly ascribed to the place where the call had its origin, would secure a subsequent lowering of the price: listen, send me a Ferrari and wrap it nicely for me: a glorious joke that cost us more than a tear, the big-eared guy who sells Ferraris and me. Papi Papikins, what a joker my Papi Pepikins is: convulsion and the compulsion to give Papi Pipikins a great big kiss. Big-eared Ferrari dealer who 'til then or till then, because both constructions are tactically or syntactically correct, just as the tactical or syntactical words or expressive forms are correct, was trying to get a lottery agency for the benefit of the aunt of the friend of the cousin of the mother of his mother-in-law. I am pleased to make a correction: the one who called was my secretary, so that the auricular presence of an intermediary would have the effect of impacting the posterior conversation and the effect on the effects that the transaction would have on my pocket. What I mean is that you're a generalized general, Papi Papikins: a wreath of compliments that Benny laid at the feet of the statue he had erected for his father. The Papi Papikins alluded to roams along the lower shore of his interior stream: why did I agree to give Benny a Ferrari? A good question deserves a good answer: to deny myself the satisfaction of rewarding him with a dialectical punch in the nose on the basis of the antagonistic ideogram sweat and tears, bliss and satisfaction.

WHAT I MEAN is that I want to give myself the tremendous ecstasy of being the first teen-ager in the country to burn gasoline in a Ferrari. Or what I mean is that a Ferrari is some kind of wild airship that, that, that, I know what I want to say but I don't know how to get it all together, that, that, that. Transcription of poor Benny's mental latticework: death to the objectivism of Robbe-Grillet and Miss Sarraute: a Ferrari is a fabulous airship that the Italian manufacturer allows to be used on highways so that it won't be said that he evades surfaces: Italians do their thing, Calabrians and Sicilians do their thing. What I mean is that it's a genuine discovery what I'm discovering, that the Ferrari is from Italy, the Pope lives in Italy and the Pope lives in the Vatican and the Vatican has diplomatic immunity. What I mean is is it immunity or impunity?, and the course in International Politics I took last semester at the University of Puerto Rico is fried come and the course of my Ferrari can't be bothered by some braking here, some braking there.

BROKEN CULVERT, SIGNAL out of order, blinker, electric gate, speed checked by Vascar system, hill, divided highway ends, slow, school zone, slippery when wet, curve, bump, detour, men working, pedestrian crossing, pavement ends, road under construction, 25 MPH, merge, speed limit forty miles per hour, do not enter, no left turn, no right turn, no U-turn, student driver, the Highway Department regrets the inconvenience.

WHAT I MEAN Papi is that the Añasco track where it is is in Añasco, that the Añasco track where it is isn't in San Juan. What I mean Papi is that the project of a law comes out of your thinking cap, out of your well-oiled brain. What I mean Papi is that if you have a well-made track where young people can get their kicks with mileage like Marysol Malaret: Puerto Rican Miss Universe and national glory by decree. What I mean Papi is that we young people will be thankful to you. What I mean Papi is what's happening is that we young people have all got moth-eaten. What I mean is that it's not so bad to hear the guaracha of that monkey-faced nigger and like it gets into something and your anger all grows cold. It all grows cold until my Ferrari is reached by that Christlovesyou that reaches.

AND LADIES AND gentlemen, friends, the rhythm that Macho Camacho has proposed, imposed, transposed, reposed, and just posed in his Olympian guaracha is truly phenomenal: a free pass to a healthy shindig: shin from shinnying up and dig from digging down into the flavor that comes out of Villa Cañona, a shindig with great big capital letters and a little cold beer.

OR DID SHE learn that life is a phenomenal thing from Macho Camacho's selfsame guaracha?, a guaracha with a devastating slogan, a guaracha that incites to permanent partying, an evangelical ode to happy happenstance: we've happened onto the Bible. There are things that are never known to be known, the mystery of the world is a world of mystery: a quotable quote. What is well known is that everything is plink to her, it's well known from her own mouth, listen to her: everything is plink to me. Listen to this other one: everything slips away from me. Lend an ear to what you hear: I can wiggle my way through anything: and, immediately, she shrugs her shoulders, twists her mouth, snorts through her nose, turns off her eyes: clichés made serious by the commonality *I don't give a whore's hard turd for anything:* her Lord's Prayer. Don't look at her now because she's looking now.

TAKE A BREAK, smoking is permitted, the tutti-frutti breath that Adams' Chiclets purvey, a short beer, a spot of coffee, let the tired person stretch his legs, the lazy person mark the page and continue reading another day, and the

one who wants to know something new watch her and
hear her now:

WHEN I WANT to enjoy, I enjoy, and sometimes I enjoy
without wanting to, psst: the fun's going to end with her. Or
if it doesn't end it will cripple her heart and soul: because of
Carolina's Nameday Party, because at Carolina's Nameday
Party I danced with a catch from Barrazas, because a bash in
La Muda, because some meat pies at the pigmeat place Here
I Stay, because we ate some blood sausages at the pigmeat place
Here We Are Again, because a veal fricassee at the El Chorrito
restaurant, because a come-as-you-are party at Mar Chiquita
beach, because an Adam and Eve party at the house of a
screwer in Ocean Park, because we went through four cases of
beer, because we downed three quarts of Don Q, because I dye
my hair, because I undye my hair, because I dye my hair again,
because the rollers, because the wig, because I'm going to tie
it up in bits of paper, because the hang, because the eyelashes,
because: it's enough for anybody.

SOMETHING, AN IMPRECISE and finally precise
something seasons her usual ugliness and converts it into a
prettiness that little by little pulls things together, the way the
chorus of a good guaracha pulls them, well bloated, well tipped,
well bellied. A whorish living off promises, do the eyes guaran-
tee a flow of ardor, the mouth that bespeaks baritone whispers
of aggressive pleasure, the tongue that anticipates the *s*'s of a

62

snake, the mounds of the breast that swear a sweet death in the nipples, and other further promises that are promised in the composite and harmonious sweat and the facility of the fuzz? Well supplied with thighs, the hips with too much Dinga or Mandinga backstitching: a chip off Grandpa, crab-fishing vendor of fresh coconuts in the almond ways of Medianía Alta; Grandpa Monche deified in family sagas anxious to be explained, epic, the narrative way, anxiousness and anxieties unleashed in Grandma Moncha's white soul and black body over Grandpa Monche's black soul and black body: proud black, loud black, dinner-table black, a sir and would you please black; Mother said that Grandma Moncha said that Grandpa Monche said: white meat is the ruination of the black man and the laughing could be heard in Medianía Baja and the laugh curled around my body like a reed and curled me up like a reed I could have turned out children by twos: Grandma Moncha's laugh, lightened and frightened by asthma. Turn after turn, five o'clock and he hasn't come and a Winston tastes good like a cigarette should, smoke in her eyes, hawking, snorting, she drives off the coughing with a shit: she's crude.

SHE'S WEARING A wedding ring, the ringed hand holds a cubalibre, a cubalibre with a double shot; the other hand, an overfed charm bracelet, scratches a thigh; the thumb, as habitual intruder, becomes dark and savage. Let us describe the conduit where the thumb is known to act as habitual intruder: membranous, fibrous, and in the female mammal it extends from the vulva to the matrix: vociferous and sententious her membranous and fibrous conduit, practical, fits well in any mouth, tolerates a considerable expansion. And placed

63

in the middle for my holy remedy, as she proverbializes: coarse, a diploma in vulgarity, practitioner and addict of the same. As on every Monday, Wednesday, and Friday afternoon, the twilight mistress, she awaits naked. Because The Old Man likes to find her in her serene skin. The Old Man doesn't say so, fine and refined as he is, gentleman and gentlemanly as he is: she makes fun, her tongue dancing a guaracha against her cheeks. The Old Man says. But he says it without leaving any tracks, his foxy talents wound up in foxiness learned in the governmental fox den: I say such an imperious necessity of finding you in the saturated empire of your roundness, I say such limpid pleasure in finding you in limpid genesis, I say such a spanning bridge is your stomach between Hispanic Antilleany and Adamic ribbery: a little recherché, a little artificial. She thinks: packages, tricks, fakes: finding me naked, period. She waits undressed, it's already been said. She waits smoking, it's already been said. Or smoking she waits for the man she loves. Lyricking by Sarita Montiel, enshawled and carnationed behind the glass of festive show windows. If she's silent she'll burst: loving him my eye.

SUCKING THE JUICE out of his pocket is what I love. Plucking him like a chicken is what I love. Hypnotizing him in the wallet is what I love. Squeezing him until he lets go of all the bills he has on top or on bottom is what I love. Sucking out his last penny is what I love. Or the next to the last. On each occasion that she makes reference to the nominative of the personal pronoun of the first person in masculine or feminine gender and singular number she punishes her corpulent teatery with fierce slaps. That's it, that's it: make something out of her dirty work: dollars, dollars, dollars: hot coals in her eyes: dollars, dollars, dollars: malefic and hair-raising: dollars, dollars, dollars: colleague of Agatha the witch: right out of the stories to calm Memo, Little Lulu's neighbor. Macho Camacho's guaracha lacquers and perfumes the apartment: in the corners, in the crannies, in the tripod with Japaneseries, in the painting with a swan in an idyllic lake, in the painting of *The Last Supper:* Judas, Judas always butting in, lets go with a little wiggle, Peter scolds him: behave yourself. The vaccination against Macho Camacho's guaracha in all national territory is highly justified; a possible press conference by a possible National Secretary of Fun: feasible in the here and now: dancing, drinking, dicing.

THE BUTTS, THREE of them, entwine a sprout of smoke that ends in an unbalanced asterisk: a clumsy attempt at a flower that falls apart: leaden sinuosities stumped by a ceiling of rough stucco that can be touched with the fingers: a reduced little lair that is a celebration of ineptness: a synthesis of kitchen, bath, living room, bedroom: a sofa that changes into a bed that changes into a sofa, a sofa of lumpy narrowness that proclaims a dogmatic and alienated law of physics: two bodies are not authorized to occupy the space reserved for one. A series of quips made by her the day she saw the apartment for the first time: but this is a penny house, this is an ounce house, this is a bargain-sale house, this is a peewee house, this is a hut for the dwarfs involved with Snow White.

NO, IT'S NOT a penny or small-change house, it's not an ounce or lightweight house, it's not a bargain-sale house, it's not a peewee house: a series of answers made by The Old Man. And in the words bargain-sale and peewee I celebrate the idea of brevity stipulated by the moving mastery of the lower classes. It's not a hut worthy of the concupiscent activities of pygmies or Lilliputians, no, no, no: no one has ever had a more flexible occipital. It's only, it's rather, it's nothing more than, it's strictly, it's specifically, it's restrictively: a furnished studio in the best tradition of humility, neither grievous nor onerous, that I utilize sporadically, that I utilize from time to time, that I utilize on occasion, that I utilize alternately in order to effect with the diligence obliged and expected of my person, post, prestige, position, the proper reflection upon the nation, which was, is, and shall be my greatest preoccupation and principal desire until the day on which the Stygian swamp sees me carried along by Charon: she didn't understand a word. A furnished studio that I utilize, in the second place in enumeration, which does not imply a second place in importance, to urge, to claim, to reclaim the generous aid of the muses and perform competently on the pages full of the flames of love of country that I read on the senatorial podium to the admiration of the majority body, the minority body, the press that comments on me and all the people who empty into the ancient and august parliamentary palace of Puerta de Tierra disposed to praise my eloquence: also there are those who say it has more clout than a brace of bombs, there are also those who say that he's too wise to say it again. This aptitude of mine that goes back to the apostrophic tirades of Caius Tullius Cassius: the forceful phrase, the lyrical idea, a style embroidered with beauty, metaphors leaping forth like a young cloudburst, malleable words, the oration whiplashy, the voice silvery, the z pronounced like a z Castilian style: besieged by pomposity. A furnished studio in the best tradition of humility that I utilize, utilize, utili, utili, uti, uti, u, u.

I'M SORRY, HEATHEN Chinky, but your nakedness plethoric with roundness and its thick fertilizer of innocent sweat sponsors in me an amorous reunion with the erogenous urges that rose into public view long years ago: with pride I declare that at the age of ten I damaged a little servant girl. With the aforesaid act I shamed the authoress of my days, who needed the spiritual attentions of a Thomasine Father. With the aforesaid act I honored the author of my days, who, surrounded by the smooth aroma of his Havana from Havana, declared: the son of a cat will catch a rat and, in recognition of such a precocious devirginizing creature, invited me to La Mallorquina for ice cream and cookies. I'm sorry, Heathen Chinky, but the casual observance of the black flowers that proclaim their innocence in the sparse gardens of your lower stomach inoculates me with the glorious bacillus of satyriasis. I'm sorry, Heathen Chinky, but I close the hermeneutic phase of our relationship and open the frolicking phase. I'm sorry, Heathen Chinky, but the big spoonful of Testiviton ingested every other morning or so keeps me the way it keeps me.

HOW DOES IT keep him? Gossip? Driveler? Faker? Sweet-talking? Eatmeup? The elevator rumbles, the door is keyed, and I take it easy, relax, ready for the flattering and the chattering and other atterings: Fine and Mellow they call me. Turn after turn, a return to the but today he's late, later than usual, later than, a reflection interrupted by an explosion of well-being: firm as a worm and higher than a papaya I line up the fifth cubalibre, I drink myself silly with banana tonic and, what the hell, I daydream about my cousins from La Cantera, rough and tough and hairy as monkeys, rough and tough and one hair short of being monkeys, rough and tough and the kind who give an order and go, rough and tough, my cousins: cousins known since the time they moved to the Calle del Fuego in the Humacao days, the Calle del Fuego where we lived, Mother, me, and my brother Regino, who I called the Korean because it was in Korea that he was carried off by the one who brought him. And like a persistent rain, the memory of her hands, small hands still, eager to harden, with democratic equity, the cousins' peepee places, two at a time the three peepee places.

AND THE FACT is, ladies and gentlemen, friends, there's nothing as titanic as a man of the people who uses the talents that God gave him and that he didn't buy at the marketplace in Río Piedras or in Bargain Town. Macho Camacho is an innate talent, the kind that doesn't have a nipple where he can suck in the Washingtons, the kind that had to suck for himself . . . skin all nicely sucked.

FULL-LENGTH BUSTS OF. Excuse the unwarranted and confused interruption, but did I hear full-length busts?, he had heard full-length busts, the things a person has to hear. Vincentian thought teletypes: stupid and proud of it. Full-length busts of Washington, Lincoln, Jefferson, and other founding titans of the Puerto Rican motherland, so that our children and our children's children can discover in the majesty of the clobbered stone. Excuse the unwarranted and confused interruption, but did I hear clobbered stone?, he had heard clobbered stone; the things a person has to hear. Vincentian thought teletypes: unsalvageable savage. Discover in the majesty of the clobbered stone the repository of our history: he affixed his signature, the back of the unsalvageable savage was his desk, he gave pats of praise on the desk of the one who was stupid and proud of it, the pats of praise opened up the effervescence compartments of the unsalvageable savage, effervesced and effervescent, they could have called him Alka-Seltzer, the one who was stupid and proud of it bounced up the steps of the ancient and august parliamentary palace of Puerta de Tierra, he bounced up the steps after wrinkling his jacket: a hug. Clasp that closes the string of annoyances: a delay for the yearned-for mistress of the moment: yearned for at the moment the insomniac animal between his legs began to fiddle around and repeat: let's go. From a meeting of the Committee for the Establishment of Responsible Citizenship: the scabrous theme requires a period of moral reflection that I want us to begin this afternoon. With the mistress of the moment: with his neatly hidden love affairs and mistresses he could form a stable: how many fillies: puffing up his cheeks like the fabled frog. Vanity, bragging, a wild hustle and bustle, a me yes and what's the matter adorn the word mistress.

THE WORD MISTRESS: and not even faces come back to him because he jots them down on this or that payroll of the Secretariat this one or that one: he's a member of the powerful legislative committee on dollars and cents. A big mulatto who spits out everything and starts singing when he sees the computer perforate a card that refers to special personnel, or emergency personnel, or temporary personnel: the Senator's last fucky-fucky appears on the payroll. The word mistress contaminates some sterile fevers, 104 degrees of sterility, which neither the dignity proclaimed nor the first-class surname nor the gentlemanliness nor the fineness nor the other notations of pedigree bother: 104 degrees of sterility: with a tentacular hand, Senator Vicente Reinosa—Vince is a prince and words doesn't mince —salutes the insomniac animal between his legs, a martial salute, certification, and he proclaims: most prudent balls, venerable balls, praiseworthy balls, powerful balls, honorable balls, balls of outstanding devotion, balls that shelter and protect. Love affair or ceremonies of illicit masonry where I reiterate my virility and its triumph: a contradiction in the language that a feminine noun should be so masculine: he chuckles and celebrates his wit as no one could celebrate it: a redundancy and fact to keep in mind: nobody admires him as much as he admires himself: at night, when he goes hunting for sleep, emulating Proust, he wonders with a perplexity that perplexes him: I wonder why I'm so big, what stuffing have they stuffed me with? The current mistress, the eightieth in his whoric algebra, looks more Philippine from the immoderate slant of her eyes, barcaroles of literary Japanishness. But the strong, dazzling, shiny darkness is from here: grown here out of Bartolomé de Las Casas' recruitments.

BARTOLOMÉ DE LAS CASAS, recruiter of black masses from Timbuktu and Fernando Po, black masses that wiggle asses, that cock it, that open their legs to white classes from Extremadura and Galicia, white classes that wiggle asses, that cock it, that open their legs to Taino lasses from Manatuabón and Otoao, Taino lasses from Manatuabón and Otoao that wiggle their asses, that cock it, that open their legs to black masses from Timbuktu and Fernando Po: fuck about, suck about, and anybody without a Dinga has got a swineherd from Trujillo and a squaw: all milks the milk: the darkskin is from here.

COLORED FEMALES HEAT me up: the worst-kept secret in the Senate: Senator Guzmán, peer of a pair of motels, with jibes and jabber accuses him of black-woman trade: colored females heat me up: he accepts the color calories with the tragic sense of life: he's an Ortegan, but he lunches on Unamuno. Chance has it that she, I say she and pronominate my concubine, my kept woman, my lover, my mistress, in her scant reflective activity, doesn't think that she regales me with, offers me, donates me, lends me, pledges me, sells me a pleasure or a good time that I, Senator Vicente Reinosa—Vince is a prince and his word will convince—can't get wherever I want, however I want, whenever I want, and in virtuous function of my multiplied genetic talents: a parable from the Book of Matthew: multiplied by the will of the being and lots of amens. So that she, I say she and: please go back to the lines above, has learned that quality isn't manufactured all wrapped up in the cellophane of a boy who has recently sprouted his feathers or a boy who has recently and clumsily given in to the confrontation of carnal pleasures. Quality is produced, succeeds, takes shape after an incessant repetition of certain acts of an experimental nature that culminate in the qualitative act, attained, shaped. Said in another way or said in street language: you've got to stick it in long and hard to stick it in well: what an expansion of my insides, what cool and what coolness there is in my interior abode. Theresus of Ávila on the horizon?

A SPECTACULARITY, THAT'S a lot of word, even better than the even more difficult ones that appear on circus posters every season: rumors that compete in being out of proportion and in trying to screw your patience: a spectacularity: doing somersaults in the breezes that blow at five in the afternoon with the spectacularity of the Flying Saucers of Ringling Brothers Circus: which doesn't mean that the light is damaged or anything like that nor the energy crisis nor what it feeds on. What it means is that a gasoline truck went out of control, jackknifed, tipped over, landed on a nice new little Volvo driven by a woman in an interesting state: the fetus rose up into her mouth. That a school bus hurt some strikers. That some strikers hurt a school bus. That a mugger mugged a paymaster: catalytic rumors of impatience that have their center of operation in the stomach: five o'clock in the afternoon on Wednesday, today Wednesday.

THERE ON THE windshield, right in place, swims his own narcissus face. Swims or floats or remains on the surface of the glass, never diving, swimming or floating when he looks and looks backward, forward, toward the sides. With the guild of trapped, tripped, tricked drivers he shares the intentions of a possible hysterical explosion but deprives himself of it, deprives himself of the consequent exterior formature of the same by what self-control is or a piece of it and his objections and dissidences must be oriented along the paths established by it. Senator Vicente Reinosa—Vince is a prince and with honor ever since—in an instant or jiffy plugs into a schoolgirl who must be round about fifteen when she gets home and washes the pound of makeup down the drain: transported by a Mazda; soap, water, and ten years that go to end in the sea, counting on the fact that the plumbing is working because if it's not: Jorge Manrique, if I saw you I no longer remember. The schoolgirl isn't calm, the schoolgirl won't be calm, the schoolgirl won't let herself be calm, the schoolgirl isn't epileptic, the schoolgirl isn't autistic, the schoolgirl hasn't got Saint Vitus. Nor does she have a hallucinating mushroom nor has she been bitten by an Amazon snake or by the black widow spider that has its poison in Ponce, nor is she inhabited by the evil-genius spirit of the Virgin of Midnight, the Virgin That's What You Are. No. The schoolgirl who must be round about fifteen when she gets home and washes the pound of makeup down the drain is won over, irretrievably won over by the cult of Macho Camacho's guaracha. The schoolgirl chews guaracha like a vile chiclemaniac until her jaws become low-keyed castanets. A pause to give the low-keyed castanets of her jaws an audience, pause, pause, pause.

SENATOR VICENTE REINOSA—Vince is a prince and his manner doesn't wince—thinks that he should worry about his fellow man, solemnities adjunct to his position: need help? Just that: need help? Impossible to tell her: let's play cat and mouse: he's fine and refined, a gentleman and gentlemanly: he chooses to smile with an accordionic smile and nods as one who proposes something. The schoolgirl shakes up the licentious and senatorial eyes that, like flies or gnats or mosquitoes, fondle her breasts and galvanize her: exactly, large breasts like breadfruits that parody the California burlesque *Mother of Eight.* The schoolgirl waves her hands, a slight wave the first time, an earthquaky wave the second, a hysterical wave the third. An inquiring shout: listen, what are you looking at me for, do I owe you something, what have I got that I'm not giving you, if it's your mistress you miss, go find her, I'm not her kiss. The response is rhymed and recited with an equivocal and ambiguous tonality that escapes the powerful antenna of Senator Vicente Reinosa—Vince is a prince and marked to convince. I can't hear you, miss, I can't hear you, separated by a wall built of blocks of Macho Camacho's guaracha, I can't hear you, I can't hear you, I can't: let it bring to mind the last scene in *La dolce vita* where Mastroianni is deaf to the call of the pigtailed adolescent, separated by a body of water, in the midst of a confessional dawn of unsheltered places, I can't hear you, I can't hear you, I can't. Although it's not a question of seeing, seeing her turn off her eyes, it's probably the generation gap, the parricide that we all partake of, the unisex style, the rage of the emerging generation, the youth today.

SENATOR VICENTE REINOSA—Vince is a prince and his mind you can't rinse—in order to drive away the shame brought on by the disdain of the schoolgirl who must be round about fifteen when she gets home and washes the pound of makeup down the drain, a shame that wraps around his soul like a strip of crepe paper, whistles. With long stretches of timidity he whistles a tune, a mock-up of the rhythm of the guaracha that has taken over the country, drunk in the country, sucked up the country. Thunder, lightning, sparks, eurekas, gollies, wows, heys, shee-eets, fuckitallium: when he becomes aware of his sudden moral fall. He looks once. Twice. Three times. In the name of God and those who abide with him: may thanks and more thanks be given: no one has noticed his fall. The schoolgirl doesn't interrupt her masticatory activity, nor does she hide it. The schoolgirl, with an open gesture, with an open gesture because it shakes her at the roots of her hair, reveres Macho Camacho's guaracha, as Macho Camacho's guaracha is revered by the hundreds of drivers who. Ashamed, saddened, crushed because he has hummed Macho Camacho's guaracha, a street-corner anthem, repulsive, high or low, a little or a lot, the guaracha: a tiara of vulgarity, a headdress of trash, a banner of the rabble, has alighted on his lips: what difference does it make if with fleeting breezes, a sin is a sin even though the time might have been used. Sinner, vulgarian, a repetition of Sunday masses, raise your sinful eyes to seek an open place, a pilgrim's meadow where you can rest them: green to calm the madness. In search of a redemption in the landscape he discovers an immense sign that says, biblical, litanical, apocalyptical:

AND LADIES AND gentlemen, friends, this man sits down one day and writes a guaracha that is the mother of all guarachas, sweet, neat, a treat. And that guaracha because it's so true is going up to the heaven of fame, into the first rank of popularity, into the repertory of every combo in the stew, the spread of every combo that's into salsa, the sauce, and a combo that's not into salsa is nowhere.

WHICH, LISTEN TO me Ciela, you won't take off even
to do the brazen copulative act. What's that Mama?, a frightened street-crossing eye to eye. That's the carnal penetration
of his privy part into yours. A dracular horror knocked Ciela
over; four arms, and an embrace and two sets of loud and
tremulous wailing combined into one solitary figure in which
terror reigned round about. Goldilocks chased by the three
bears didn't suffer as much, neither King Kong in love nor the
Wolf Man aroused by the critical consciousness of his felony
suffered a thing if all their suffering were compared to the
smallest fraction of Ciela's suffering. Ciela, Graciela, her head
nestled on the lungs of her widowed mother, imagined her
body run through by an evil meat-slicing gaucho knife that
would emerge from his unmentionable place. Her hair, the
little stream of rouge, the chain with the savior crucifix, her
Swiss airs snowy and pure, all fell away from her. She spat out
snot and sobs and fear and wonder: a lava of emotions and
anonymous homage to Etna. And from her mouth a gelatinous
humor, gelatinous like a stew of Chinese soup, Chinese eggdrop soup. And through her nose. Her widowed mother: a
picador without a horse: you weren't refined in Switzerland
snowy and pure in order to return to Puerto Rico just to do that
thing. With moral repugnance she pronounced the neuter
object and tied it with the cords of a sacred disgust. The house
on the Calle Luchetti, a peak-roofed house with a mango tree,

sold. The overhang in Barranquitas with a stand of Congo banana trees, sold. The six cows with radiant udders, sold. The painting *Bords de Seine* by Frasquito Oller, sold. Even my deathbed candle sold so that in Switzerland snowy and pure you would be a solvent and respected pupil in spite of your coming from an island that Isabella and Ferdinand, for León and for Castile a whole New World did Columbus steal, shouldn't have authorized for settlement and should have agreed for it to be a principality of mosquitoes and a place of retirement for those on fixed incomes: so embracing the embrace that it hurt them and they let go: orphaned of her father almost from birth but never straying from the exclusive path that ends at the knees of God the Papa. They massaged themselves with a lotion of cherubic smiles and intoned a miniature hymn. A mystical fragrance, a scent of I stood and I forgot, a flood of angelic crab lice made everything hazy.

MY CIELA, I know that you really are Ciela made celestial forever, worthy of pregnancy by a holy spirit or a generous sylph: widow-maternal prolegomena to the apostrophe that follows: with the courage of a creature decanted with decency in her veins, leave the place of sin to the whims of the breeze. So you close your eyes and with a voice inaudible to the man, but powerful and appealing to the guardian seraphs, you begin to say the prayer God Save You Queen and Mother. The beast that dozes in all men will awaken in your man at the offering of the restless sin. Shouts of pleasure, grunts of sick delight will come from his throat, the whinnying of lascivious contentment and an occasional foul and stinking fart. You deaf to it all, my

Ciela; dead like a corpse to it all, my Ciela; alive only for the God Save You Queen and Mother, Mother of Mercy, my Ciela.

THE STOP AT the pharmacy in Quebradillas to buy a refill of citron water. In Bayamón she had consumed the first jug. From Bayamón to Manatí she didn't say a peep. In Manatí she took two Cortals and with an artificial relaxation announced, singing and trilling like an announcer for Colgate: *Cortal, when taken, stops the achin'.* From Manatí to Arecibo she didn't say boo. Once in Arecibo she opened her mouth again to proclaim with great wisdom: *Arecibo is Captain Correa's town* and to the genteel approval of her husband repeated, merry, witty, jovial, talkative: *Cortal, when taken, stops the achin'.* A memory of the slow sea of Guajataca transformed into a plowed field of blue by her husband's rampant vulgarity. A memory of the adobe cottage where they stayed, transformed into a doll's house denied to Ibsen by her husband's rampant vulgarity. A memory of going down to the beach at Guajataca, transformed into a promenade of clay and flamboyants by her husband's rampant vulgarity. A memory of the solemn and immaculate chasteness of the camisole of monkish cut and austere lace that you won't take off even to do the brazen copulative act. A piercing memory of the scream she gave off when her husband got undressed and in the darkness she saw the gleam as if from an evil meat-slicing gaucho knife that emerged from his unmentionable place. Screaming: the hotel man came, the hotel woman came. Screaming: the police from the Quebradillas, Isabela, and Aguadilla precincts came. The hotel woman said:

that one won't be mounted tonight and yawned. A memory that a month after the wedding, settled now in the big house on the Paseo de Don Juan, they did the brazen copulative act.

GRACIELA DRAPES HERSELF with a cloak of memories as the receptionist adduces: the excessivity of cold is causified in her by the neatisity of our conditioner of airs. Hadn't the psychiatrist told her when he was hiring her that she should choose, weigh, and measure her words because a psychiatrist's clientele was very upper-crust, high-toned, mainly hoity-toity, and faithful payers of the forty dollars an hour for couch and ear? A psychiatrist's clientele: fabulous fauna of fabulists: frustration for the frustrated fruit, depression, my capacity to recognize my incapacity, my dreams of falls from high places, a nightmare about a zebu bull that chases me, the country works an unworkable effect on my psyche, the trauma of my unconscious because the consensus in the country produces an I don't know what that brings on in me a what do I know, the narrowness of the means, the mental fatigue of Sundays and. Look how:

DOCTOR SEVERO SEVERINO leaning against a window bitten by Atlantic waves attacks the expositive aria of his trade. Doctor Severo Severino is well-built, a touch of the mature Italian, Raf Vallone type, Rossano Brazzi type: handsome as he is, skin perpetually bronzed by the sun he drinks in at his house on the beach amidst matchbooks that he collects from all over the world and pictures of actors from silent movies that he collects: roaring twenties with Clara Bow, with Theda Bara, with Gloria Swanson, with Pola Negri, with Ramon Novarro, with Vilma Banky, with Anna May Wong, with Charlie Chaplin and Buster Keaton: minimanias that compensate for some deficiency or small disadvantage that, the aria:

THE DANGER CONSISTS in the fact that the psychiatrist might cut off the ballocks of the patient's heart. But, besides and on all sides, so many repairs and miracles are expected of a psychiatrist, so many recuperations, so much stitching woven with the discharge of guilt. Because you get rid of shitty guilt and relief gets inside. The miracle consists in the psychiatrist's tearing off the blindfold that covers the fucking guilt, breaking the hymen of the guilt. The leap from tribal witch doctor to metropolitan witch doctor has been tolerable: from chewing coca to a nickel's worth of Freud.

WITH WELL-DISSEMBLED dissembling, the receptionist watches Graciela shrug: I wouldn't listen to her talk for hours on end, I'd stick a brush in one hand, a cake of blue soap in the other, and a basin of dirty clothes between her two legs: nerves or not, she can't fool me, crazy like they say, she doesn't look it: crazy as a coot, she doesn't look it: neurotic like they say, she doesn't look it, she hasn't chewed a single nail, she's got them all nice and long and well taken care of: she does look skinny. She is skinny: a thinness called for by obese modistes who chase away obesity, hair fixed with lacquered naturalness, mounted on whitened legs, arms dolled up with bracelets, and rings, and hoops. Of course, the psychiatrist says that the rich and the not so rich who want to shit higher than their ass are colored by different realities and are measured by what's inside. But since I don't know what they eat it all leaves me cold as a cake of ice. As far as I'm concerned, rich ladies and the ones who aren't rich but want to pass themselves off as rich have got their heads mixed up with their asses.

GRACIELA CONTEMPLATES THE immense X-ray picture that covers the wall. The reduction to a bony nightmare is repulsive for what it has of proven prophecy: her unpublished profundity surprises her: she's read *Love Story* three times, she subscribes to *Vanidades, Harper's Bazaar,* and *House and Garden:* for some time she's wanted to sink her teeth into something by Enrique Laguerre or René Marqués: people in our own backyard are God's children too: objective, democratic, well put together: if the backyard people weren't so pessimistic and tragical: forget slums, forget Puerto Rican independence, forget characters who sweat: everything that's written should be refined and elevated, literature should be refined and elevated. The receptionist hands her the latest *Time.* Graciela glances through the latest *Time.* With horror and disgust Graciela turns over some snapshots from napalmized Vietnam reproduced in the latest *Time* because she can't tolerate anguish even for a minute: nothing painful, nothing mournful, nothing miserable, nothing sad: I wasn't born for that. Graciela pauses fas-ci-na-ted, en-chan-ted, be-wit-ched, to look at the fascinating, enchanting, bewitching photograph of Liz and Richard's house in Puerto Vallarta: typical and topical:

86

a nostalgic mansion from the times of Don Porfirio, bougainvillaea and prickly-pear cactus limbs in whose skeletal shade peasant women make tortillas, tortillas cooked in a clay dish as red as the earth from which it was made, menacing petroglyphs of Tlaloc and Quetzalcoatl resting on the balcony, on the corner a hand-organ with a musical roll of *Adelita*. A hundred sighs later, nauseated from the swaying of her thoughts, Graciela turns another page and: oh, oh, oh, oh: the Donald Duck tantrum.

AND THOSE LYRICS, ladies and gentlemen, friends, those religiously inspired lyrics, those lyrics that speak truths, those lyrics that speak realities, those lyrics that speak of things the way they are and not the way you want them to be. Because, come on, ladies and gentlemen, friends, who's going to argue the argument with me that life isn't a phenomenal thing?

"HOW ABOUT THAT, " said The Mother, her head no, no. "The fun it is to have a ball," said The Mother, her head yes, yes. "When that guaracha says that life is a phenomenal thing, that's when my brain goes wildest," said The Mother, feet together with a halted turn and a wiggle of the waist and movements that bespoke merriment and sprees. "The day when Iris Chacón sings and dances Macho Camacho's guaracha will be the day to end all days," said The Mother, her lower lip bitten by her upper teeth and her lower teeth, her head no, no, her head yes, yes. "The Lord protect us on that day," said Doña Chon, cleaning a doll dressed up in Sevillian costume, occupying the same armchair for two years, a very ugly doll, wrinkles and moles, a doll that was regal in her occupation of the chair. "On that day Iris Chacón will have to hire a whole convoy of bodyguards or take on six black belts, because on that day they'll eat her raw," said The Mother. "Raw," repeated The Mother and made the word explode bingety-bang. Doña Chon took an oath, the sign of the cross traveled to her temple, her navel, her right shoulder, her left shoulder: The Celestial Father must be up to here with so much indecency. Doña Chon brushed away the breadcrumb stuck to the most holy feet of Saint Expeditus with a piece of flannel cloth, a crumb adjacent to the glass of water from which Saint Expeditus drank. "Iris Chacón's flesh is natural flesh," said The Mother, a beautiful swaying of hands and the cheeks of her ass fed by the floor and bits and pieces of Macho Camacho's guaracha as it crept through the thin walls. "Because Iris Chacón doesn't use silicone, no sir, the way other musical and vaudeville singers use silicone," said The Mother, a hurricane-driven windmill at the ribs, a vortex at the fingers. Doña Chon, her nose winnowing with a snort of mistrust, a crown of inquisitorial smoke, rigid as a little Spanish priest, Saint Expeditus' glass of water squeezed like an orange press, straddling a chair that straddled the armchair that the ugly doll dressed Sevillian style had occupied for two years: what's silicone? The Mother, her lips pursed in the shape of a little heart, the uncultivated voce of a diva, the voce of María Félix in *The Crag of Lost Souls*, rubbing her thighs; Ninón Sevilla style, Meche Barba style, María Antonieta Pons style, Dolly Sisters style, Amalia Aguilar style, Tongolele style, Isabel Sarli style, Libertad Lamarque style, Evelyn Souffront style, Iris Chacón style: silicone is a medicine that was put together so women like us can make our busts and hips grow bigger. Doña Chon gathered all the fright of the world together in a frightful exclamation: "How awful!" Horrified, the discoverer of the continent of unknown obscenities Christophera Colomba, she forgot to give water to thirsty Saint Expeditus, she destraddled the chair that straddled the armchair that the ugly doll dressed Sevillian style had occupied for two years, and went to the stove to stir the pot of curds and blood sausage to be sent in one batch to the striking taxi drivers, invoking punishments and examples and marks and remarks that the world is coming to an end: amidst the gloried notes of Macho Camacho's guaracha: a permanent guest in her house.

LIKE A REPTILE marked by scales and sudden sores; like a reptile disjointing its fluted tail: slowness, clumsiness: like a reptile stirring, standing up and opening its legs wide apart, vomit and drool going down, vomit and drool running down, the eyes a gift to the swarm of flies, a swarm of flies that embroiders him a mantle and halo like an Idiot Child of the Flies: the idiocy awake, awake and enlivened by buckets of more drool and more rheum: in the middle of an islet which abandonment turns green: waving legs and slipping and falling and falling and falling: fallen and vomiting up the tail of another lizard.

"THIS AFTERNOON IT'S my trick," said The Mother, unable to hold back a belch, her mouth wiped with her sleeve, the lilies of the mangrove swamp observed, the flowers of the sargasso. "In your place I'd take a good laxative of castor oil," said Doña Chon as she emptied a dish of green bananas. "I'm going to take one of those laxatives that come in the form of candy," said The Mother as she removed a lizard drowned in The Kid's drool, cleaned the puddle of drool from The Kid's nose. The Kid was nodding. "Who would have thought of all those niceties," said Doña Chon as she threw the curds into a huge pot and the sausages into a lard can. "Laxatives in candy, injections to fatten behinds, sun baths," said Doña Chon as she took the chopper out of a straw bag and cleaned it: signs of contrariness and surprise, the expressive tone of I won't say a word. "Sun baths," said Doña Chon, her head no, no. A high fever is what it's going to give him: physician and prophetess. A bad sunstroke is what it's going to give him: wise woman and seer. In the pretty little hole of his pretty little ass a little boil is going to boil up: reiterative and Mita of La Cantera, María Lionza of Venezuela, María Sabina Aztec mushroom woman. "The sun will burn away his mushiness," said The Mother as she shooed the flies with a flannel rag.

"The sun will drive away his boobishness," said The Mother. The Mother was scratching the stubborn wires of her armpit. "The sun like an onion will beg your pardon and do its best to give you a hard-on," said The Mother. The Mother's eyes, hanging one from another like bad acrobats, leap and inspect and bump and run over The Kid's big head.

THE KID IS having his sun bath now, surrounded now, surrounded by the mob that found a perfect toy in his imbecility: a toy that cries, that moans, that huddles, a toy lost and found in the little park on the Calle Juan Pablo Duarte on the hurried afternoon of a domestic April: a child, some child or other, a warlike Launcelot on a charging tricycle, asked him what's the matter? when he saw him look, watched him look, through a noose of drool that was taking shape on the very tip of his tongue, at an Indian file of ants. The question didn't get anywhere. The question floated for a second and then became a part of the zone of the forgotten. The question what's the matter? The child, some child or other, the warlike Launcelot on a charging tricycle, asked again with an impatience fortified by the ingestion of vitaminic complexes and Scott's emulsion. Also asking what's the matter again was a freckleface, the spit and image of a guardian devil, who enriched his volatile image with an excited hoot. He was also asked what's the matter by a little girl with eat-me-up teeth. It could have been the drool or the springlike eyes or the body entrenched in the body that produced the discovery. A herd being pursued doesn't move as fast as the disbelieving voices that shouted, happily: HE'S AN IDIOT, the capital letters sparkling with a great rejoicing that was the vessel of many great rejoicings. They clapped their hands, they pinched each other, they made a loud round of Macho Camacho's guaracha *Life Is a Phenomenal Thing,* the majority offered to tease him, the girl with the eat-me-up teeth announced that there was an empty cage at her house where she could keep him but corrected herself: where we could all keep him: altruistic, unselfish, I asked Santa Claus for an idiot but he didn't bring me one: reasoning, healthy, breakfasted on corn flakes, Libby's pear juice, chocolate milk, and ham and eggs.

THEY BROUGHT STICKS and branches, they poked him, bit him, urinated on him, stomps, faces, laugh, laugh, laugh. And a multisonic accompaniment of Macho Camacho's guaracha reduced now to a perverse ring-around-a-rosy: an apotheotic symphony of cruelty. The Kid was motionless as he distilled an infinite and protesting snort that broke out of his throat wrapped up in weeping. Doña Chon, full of grimaces and blessed is the wart of thy womb, sewer of cancer, and blessed art thou among women living in Martín Peña Channel, came to get him, came to rescue him, coming and rescuing too late because Tutú's lawyer came to her with some blah-blah and preaching and a help me out more often Doña Chon I've got six bellies to maintain.

"I CAN'T SWALLOW it and I won't swallow it and if they sweeten it for me with syrup I won't swallow it. I

can't swallow those sun baths and cheer over them," said Doña Chon. Doña Chon was searching with her hand on the top shelf of the cupboard: a little bottle where she kept her safety pins. "Well, I've noticed a change," said The Mother, the rollers in the tenderness of her lap. "A little more like tougher," said The Mother. The Mother was counting the rollers in the tenderness of her lap. "A little less like weak," said The Mother, taking a hair or two from the last roll of the rollers, blowing on them. "It breaks my heart to see him laying on the grass," said Doña Chon. Doña Chon was getting the little bottle where she kept her safety pins. "Like an ox laying on the grass," said Doña Chon. Doña Chon was putting the little bottle of safety pins on the dining-room table, the oilcloth cover. "A dog comes by and sniffs him," said Doña Chon. Doña Chon was looking for what she wasn't finding on the top shelf of the cupboard, a top shelf where living together in easy harmony were three fake cats decorated with little red apples and a real cat: inconsiderate faker, afraid of mice, Cuddles the cat, cuddled as if it were one of Rosario Ferré's knick-nacks: what a cat, breakfasting on codfish cakes, what a cat, fat cat, rogue cat. "Well, if a dog comes by and sniffs him then The Kid will learn what a dog's sniff is like," said The Mother. The Mother was untangling her hair, dividing it into equal parts to start making the rolls. "There are children in the park who play with The Kid," said The Mother. The Mother was wetting the handle of the comb. "What do you mean, play?" said Doña Chon. Doña Chon kept her loose change in the fake cats. "Unless you mean that getting a whack on the chops here, a whack on the neck there is playing," said Doña Chon. Doña Chon hefted the fake cats in order to calculate the amount of loose change. "The Kid probably gets in his whacks too." said The Mother. The Mother was making the first roll.

"*THE KID PROBABLY* gets in his whacks too," argued The Old Man whose Mistress The Mother was. "A defensive whack is the ideal whack," argued The Old Man whose Mistress The Mother was. "That's the way it is among playful kids his age," argued The Old Man whose Mistress The Mother was. "He won't let himself be devoured," argued The Old Man whose Mistress The Mother was. "In that way his limited intelligence gets a sense of belonging and being part of a group," argued The Old Man whose Mistress The Mother was. "Besides, it's good and healthy for him to take sun baths as soon as possible," argued The Old Man whose Mistress The Mother was. "Sun baths?" said The Mother. "Don't hand me that," said The Mother. "A hot fever is what it'll give him," said The Mother. "A bad sunstroke is what it'll give him," said The Mother. "In the pretty little hole of his pretty little ass a little boil is going to boil up," said The Mother. "Bah," argued The Old Man whose Mistress The Mother was "Tut," argued The Old Man whose Mistress The Mother was. "Old wives' tales beyond the consideration of science," argued The Old Man whose Mistress The Mother was. "The foolish primitivism of people who oppose reason with superstition," argued The Old Man whose Mistress The Mother was. "Exposure to the sun's rays is absolutely beneficial for the skin exposed," argued The Old Man whose Mistress The Mother was. "Sun baths are among the most ancient forms of therapy," argued The Old Man whose Mistress The Mother was. "In

France before the Republic they used sun baths as a cure for benign lunatics," argued The Old Man whose Mistress The Mother was. "Benign lunatic is the psychic category to which The Kid belongs," argued The Old Man whose Mistress The Mother was.

BECAUSE, LADIES AND gentlemen, friends, what Macho Camacho has put into his guaracha is his soul, that heart of his that's also the great heart of a man who's gone hungry. Yes, ladies and gentlemen, friends, gone hungry the way a man does who's sweaty and poor and bears the mark of the color of sufferance. Because he's no mulatto, black is what he is, pitch black and let's leave it at that.

WHAT I MEAN Papi is that if you could build a well-built track where young people can get their kicks with mileage of the Marysol Malaret type: Puerto Rican Miss Universe and even a national glory by decree of the Barbizon School of Modeling and a thriving, cheating telephone and down the burning Antillean street, swindle after swindle, between two rows of black faces. What I mean Papi is that we young people will be grateful to you. What I mean Papi is that what's happening is that we young people have got our hearts all moth-eaten because old people have set themselves up never to leave this life and we young people have got to give them a shove. What I mean is so what if a person listens to the guaracha by that monkey-faced nigger and like it gets something into you and your being mad about this traffic jam grows cold. Cold until my Ferrari is reached by that Jesuslovesyou in the beige cassock, his head shaved, Jesuslovesyou or the mother mess he asks for in the name of Jehovah, cold until my Ferrari is reached by that rehabilitated addict who asks in the name of Halfway Houses help us build a Halfway House in every town in the country: half the country smoking and shooting up: what I mean is don't ask me for anything because I'm not the giving kind.

THE GUARACHA BY that monkey-faced nigger and like it gets something into you. What I mean is I'm not a music buff. What I mean is I'm a car buff. What I mean is that business about life being a phenomenal thing is like a science that's got its pros and cons but I'm not the kind of a guy to let my head go all mushy and start philosophizing about that philosophy: what I mean is that my thing is trouble second and Ferrari first. What I mean Papi, Papikins, Pepikins, Pipikins, Popikins, Pupikins. What I mean is that I can see that the situation the country is in is sputtering. What I mean is that it's taking shape in Puerto Rico and it could even be now or in just a little while. Because the workers want to be rich and the rich people don't want to be workers because the rich people are rich. What I mean is that the rich people are smoothy-smooth, which means that the rich people are what they are. What I mean is that so many strikes do harm and hurt things: he didn't add like on a night on the town because Benny, poor Benny, insipid Benny, insoluble Benny.

HE'S GOT A virgin heart: intolerable virginity. It so happens that Benny has a chest where nothing has happened since his paps happened to him in his fetal period. Fifteen years later a hair happened, one. Believe me, I know him: Benny or inner callousness, Benny or the boy hardened over by indifference and antipathy. A puerile example: Benny has never sung in the shower in order to take his mind off the coldness of the water. Nor in the bus that was taking a graduating class to Luquillo did he sing the plena *What a Beautiful Flag,* the plena *Mama, the Bishop's Here.* But, impossible: Benny wasn't a part of any graduating class even though he graduated. Benny hasn't sung *Nights on the Town* because Benny hasn't sung any boleros.

Benny doesn't know the title of any bolero. Benny doesn't know what it is not to know. Benny doesn't know that he doesn't know a bolero softly crumbled by Rubén Escabí's hands with bohemian charm on nights of rum and beer at the bar that was like a retreat on the corner of the Callejón de la Capilla: he doesn't have eardrums for the soft and the rhythmical. Benny doesn't know that he doesn't know rhythmical joy, a joy sliced up like a large loaf of bread. Benny doesn't know that he doesn't know a poem by Neruda, soft and rhythmical, turned loose to the whims of the wind by Samuel Molina on some midnight at the café La Tea: abandoned like docks at dawn: what I mean is how much does that get you to eat, a poem by Palés Matos, a poem by Julia, a poem by Corretjer: what I mean is.

TO REPEAT, VIRGIN heart, add heart uninhabited by the miracle of being alive: saccharine but exact. Uninhabited by anguish, by true rage, by tenderness. A dream or a dreamy glow, but nothing. A living dream, a dream crouching in the eyes like a living dream, crouching in the eyes of the boys and girls who shout and sell *Claridad* and *La Hora,* indifferent to the car that squeals its tires and flees: *go to Cuba, you goddamned commie.* Even less the tremulous and deep dream of the boys and girls who meet at the café La Tahona to applaud the Trio Integración, to applaud Silvia Del Villard. A living dream, a tremulous dream, or the aggressive transparency that changes or ranges across the faces listening to Mari Bras speak: dazzled because history is inviting them to take that trip: Mari Bras speaks and they thrust out their chests toward morning because the building of freedom is talking to them through her hands; faces that disarm the night with posters, faces made fraternal with hatred for Nixon and Pinochet. But Benny: oh no. Benny is a pig. Benny is a little closet rogue for whom all abnegation is crap: what I mean is that being a revolutionary and other kinds of shithead is jerking off with a wet hand: what I mean is that I'm a wash-and-wear kind of guy: didn't I tell you?

BENNY DIDN'T ATTEND the University of Puerto Rico this semester, or the one before. Benny would stick his books into the trench of his armpit and was sure that knowledge would come to him through the phenomenon of osmosis: no sweat! Example: Benny, scared because he has a final exam tomorrow morning, deposits himself tonight in the Reference Room of the Main Library of the University of Puerto Rico: what I mean is that if *Don Quixote* comes in a family-size résumé twenty pages long why should I spend the rest of my life reading the real thing: what I mean is that I learned as a child that books stay and people leave, what I mean is that I'm not a grind, what I mean is that I'm a cool cat, what I mean is that in the sixth grade they used to call me Benny Kool-Aid. Benny would go home with his pockets full of Ds and Fs: Benny's Mami would say: before we give a donation to restore that altar at Our Lady of Grace this silly business of grades will have to be settled: that's why I'm all in favor of an elegant Parent-Teacher Association for University Children. Papi Papikins said: set a date and organize a get-together of teachers in your Mama's molto bello gardeno: a get-together with uniformed waiters, cold cuts from La Rotisserie, barrels of Beaujolais and sparkling Lambrusco: a get-together that I'll pay for through my expense account for senatorial representation. What I mean is that the teachers at the University of Puerto Rico are against me; what I mean is that the University of Puerto Rico is a big fake, a trashcan full of little cards. What I mean is that you have to copy so much that your hand gets tired. What I mean is compositions about Phoenicians who invented the art of salting fish, big fat books, and some teachers even want a person to think. What I mean is I think that if a person thinks he loses his thinking and then how is he supposed to think about what's left to think about? What I mean is that the University of Puerto Rico is controlled by FUPI independentists, marxists, communists, castroists, maoists, so many that I've lost track of them, which is why I have to backtrack to the track.

WHAT I MEAN is where the hell did that midget of a car driven by a little nigger of a driver come from: you can do it in a Volkswagen; that cockroach of a car that's cockroached up to the left rear tire of my car of cars. Ferrari old buddy: what's the story, Ferrari old buddy: tell that Volkswagen not to mess with you because this is messing with me. What I mean is do you dare? Would the Ferrari dare monoxidate its rear enemy or ask it what have I got to make you want to be such a good friend? What I mean is that now I did get myself hung up. What I mean is that I can't take my foot off the brake not even to scratch the tip of my prick. What I mean is what kind of a boxing match does that heap want. What I mean is that

Volkswagen's got some nerve and the little nigger driver had better watch what he's doing. What he's doing is letting go of the reins to try and touch the two-ton ass of a little nurse who's put the two-ton ass in his face: almost. What I mean is what the hell is going on up front that the cars don't. What I mean is that this street is so and that midget of a car wants to pass me. What I mean is what does he want: shouted. Sapristi: abracadabra of Hercule Poirot: another midget is clinging to the right rear tire of my car of cars and: a bunch of shits and more shits, a string of fucks and more fucks: behind the Ferrari, as if it were a long wedding procession, two dozen Volkswagens are lined up: if Benny read the newspapers he would have found out.

WHAT I MEAN Papi is that my thing is to have my Ferrari feel at home in Puerto Rico, my thing is for my Ferrari to have a fine environment in Puerto Rico, my thing is for my Ferrari not to get any complexes because it doesn't have, because it hasn't got the autostrada that was built for the smooth flow of Ferraris by the immortal Benito Mussolini: heard and celebrated in fascist classrooms: there was a lot of dissension on the part of this or that nobleman, wounded because his coat of arms couldn't get by the test of the *Almanach de Gotha,* there was a lot of disloyalty on the part of this or that very distant relative of Claretta Petacci. But the substantive and adjective work is there for all to see, but the substantive and adjective splendor of eternal Rome saved by the Duce is there for all to see: the fact that Luigi Pirandello was a fascist proves the moral solvency of fascism, the narrow fact that Ezra Pound was a fascist proves the moral solvency of fascism. Fellini, Bertolucci, Moravia: pagliacci, bambolotti, cocchi di mamma.

BENNY SPENDS HIS mornings in the meticulous polishing of his Ferrari. A detailed care with attent attention to the fenders, the windshields, the horns, the hubcaps, the hood: attent attention with ammonia for the chrome, wax for the body, vacuum cleaner for the seats, whisk broom for the corners inaccessible to the vacuum. The great task comes to an end when the body gives off knife-blades of glow all over the carport. Benny has lunch in the everyday dining nook set up in an extra corner of the large kitchen: wicker and crystal and big baskets of freshly picked fruit and a pair of metal shakers. The everyday dining nook set up in the kitchen is separated from the grillwork of the carport that holds three automobiles by a window frame that holds thirty or forty venetian-blind slats: what I mean is that I like my Ferrari to see me eat, what I mean is that I like to offer spoonfuls of food to my Ferrari. What I mean is that my Ferrari tells me it doesn't want anything to eat because the Ferrari's got a tiger in its tank: he hiccups, his cheeks red, he laughs. Benny spends his afternoons taking the Ferrari from San Juan to Caguas and from Caguas to San Juan. Benny spends his nights going to bed, covering up, and praying.

OUR FERRARI WHICH art in the carport, hallowed be Thy Name. Lying in a very wide double bed, reflected in a mirror that adorns a long wall, Benny discovers the soft nakedness of his body: thin surplus folds around his waist, a body that predicts layers of fat when doubled up. Rubbing and dubbing, playing with balls, like someone who doesn't want the thing he flattens his thighs. Erection ready, Benny places a copy of yesterday's *El Mundo* on the edge of the bed. Thumpy, thumpy, thumpy: ahhhhhhhhh.

AND LADIES AND gentlemen, friends, the most un-measurably popular person is Macho Camacho himself, a person who's got the fever to stay on top, a person who sets out to look at life from nearby and from far off and life seen from nearby and seen from far off is, is, is, how can I say it in a way that what I say says what life is. Well, ladies and gentlemen, friends, I'm no Macho Camacho, he's a philosopher of the feelings that you feel. But I've got the feeling of clinging to life, of the life of a down-and-outer.

I GET WORKED up thinking about my cousins from La Cantera, rough and tough, as hairy as monkeys, one hair short of being monkeys, jungle toughs, rough and tough and the kind who give an order and go, juicy my cousins: cousins known, ooh whee, since the time they came to the Calle del Fuego where we lived in the Humacao days, me, Mother, and my brother Regino, who I called The Korean because it was in Korea that he was carried off by the one who brought him: piles of Rican Reginos atomized in Korea and Vietnam, who would ever believe the story of the here and now: dark, smiling people: the line from Guillén.

AND LIKE A persistent rain, the slow surprise of a memory swollen with memories: a fragment of a memory of acrobatics on thigh trapezes, a fragment of a memory of rope-walking on knees, a Kodak memory of her hands still little hands eager to harden, with democratic equity, the peepee places of her cousins, two at a time the three peepee places: thumpy, thumpy, thumpy, thumpy: with the doggedness of someone making homemade ice cream, a dogged thumpy

thumpy so that not a single one of the cousins' peepee places should abandon its noble position of a peepee place on parade or parading, a thumpy thumpy under the house on stilts, a thumpy thumpy for the passengers on the sloop *Come with Me*, a thumpy thumpy for a pleasure that was the hope of pleasures: six years old: she and the cousins wrapped in a gloomy darkness, she and the cousins indifferent to the hen huddled down to brood twelve chicks, she and the cousins forgetting about bats and batshit blindness, two at a time the three peepee places: she wore her hair in curls and her curling up made the democratic equity of the task difficult, made it difficult but didn't stop it: not a congenital whore; although, perhaps, generously congenital with her congenital powers.

SHE'S A TRAVELER who passes between different times, cutting cane like the rig they call a scorpion, trampling on the underbrush, devastating like Dora, walking along the street with a small waist like Ofelia the Brown-Skinned Girl, fair as a hare, higher than a papaya and: shit it's five o'clock and The Old Man hasn't come. Other times I couldn't care plink if he came or didn't come or came late but today I want him to come when he's supposed to come: to set the stage the way The Old Man likes us to, anisettize his tool and suck his anisettized tool. Whatever he wants us to do so he'll loosen up and toss some extra dough my way and buy a linoleum and cover the floor that looks so. The fact is that Martín Peña Channel: wind from trumpets, imperial parade of trumpets, entrance of Macho Camacho's voice: *frontwards or backwards, however you swing:* she enjoys the penetration of Macho Camacho's guaracha.

HIGHER THAN A papaya: a hermetic simile, lining up the fourth cubalibre, the sixth cubalibre, the eighth: no one could say that she downs them by pairs, she downs them by threesomes if they let her, she's got a long and combative tolerance. Sooo happy, slappphappy: she nationalizes the *z* as she talks and comes face to face with a surfeit of *s*'s, I gorge myself on banana tonic, I serve myself a can of sausages, I swallow down a can of minced ham: prim. And, wow, look where, like someone spitting without moving a finger or flickering a lash, I gave the daydream of the century to my cousins from La Cantera who I've got a bimonthly arrangement with for that: the little tongue carrying filthy insinuations peeps out on the upper lip; from that Oriental castle garden it sends news of contentment to little Chinese eyes that shut with surprise: little tongue and little Chinese eyes react to an orthodoxy of pleasure countersigned by the calendar that Monroe posed for when she wasn't Monroe: her skirt lifted by a gust of wind that comes up out of a sewer, have you seen it?, a calendar sought by Joe DiMaggio in order to carry out a public ceremony of bonfiery exorcism, they say he hired Yankee Stadium: but nobody got rid of his masturbatory fantasies. The cousins from La Cantera: cousins with protuberant bicepation, talky, gabby, funners and Mama you're so good and Mama what have you got: verbal attacks that pay high and very high dividends: opinion of the rough and tough cousins from La Cantera who improve their sharpy trade by reading the monthly *Sexology*, weekly visits to movie theaters, the Miramar, the Rialto, and the New San Juan and the comparison of individual results: I suck her ear before asking her if she wants the steak, if she wants the sparkle on the buckle, if she wants a brooch: you tell me if they're not lowlife cousins, I'll tell you that in the crop of cousins there are lowlifes too.

A SELECTIVE DEGLOSSING of the daydream she gave her cousins from La Cantera who she's got a bimonthly arrangement with for that: a sequence of the three toughs cut off at the waist in the manner of photos used on identity cards: faggy shirts, dark glasses, heads tilted. Cut. A sequence of the three toughs lying on a bed covered with a speckled spread, a bed covered with a chenille spread, a bed covered with a patchwork spread. Across from the beds covered with a speckled spread, a chenille spread, a patchwork spread, a calendar from La Taza de Oro bar, Trujillo Alto, Puerto Rico. Camera on the face of the oldest tough: thick beard, operatic sideburns escaped from the chorus of parasols of *Luisa Fernanda,* big Pancho Villa mustache, eyes bursting with desire. Quick swing of the camera to the parts of the oldest tough; stations covered: paps buried in a tangle of hair, navel buried in a tangle of hair, pudenda buried in a tangle of hair. Cut. Sequence of the oldest tough in Everestic escalation of the authoress of the daydream. Cut. Intermittent takes of the humor called sweat pouring out of the pair's pores. Cut. Close-up of a sweating pore. Cut. Close-up of a sweating pore. Cut. Scorching shot of the oldest tough as he slices in two the membranous and fibrous conduit that extends from the vulva to the matrix of the authoress of the daydream. Cut. A panoramic shot of bodies in culminating convulsion: special interest in the rubbing of bellies: navel to navel: that's what you call fucking. Cut. Shot of the oldest tough's body as he bicycles with marathonic agility on the body of the authoress of the daydream. Cut. A panoramic shot of the body of the authoress of the daydream, slippery body, vaselined body, body oiled with Coppertone suntan lotion, body oiled with Johnson hair spray. Cut. Final shot of the hand of the authoress of the daydream during the execution of desperate and despairing caresses of the Tarzanic mane of the oldest tough. Note: repeat the reading of the previous scene after substituting middle tough and youngest tough for oldest tough: the rough and tough cousins from La Cantera are identical triplets, the difference in age is computed on the basis of minutes, there is no phallic difference whatever. When her daydream is edited, let Macho Camacho's guaracha *Life Is a Phenomenal Thing* be used as incidental and accidental music, the cousins are named Hughie, Louie, and Dewey: precisely, Uncle Itchy got it from a Donald Duck cartoon.

COUSINS KNOWN EVER since they arrived on the Calle del Fuego, during the Humacao days, where she, Mother, and her brother Regino lived. First cousins on Mother's side, sons of Mother's younger brother, sons of Uncle Itchy: known as Uncle Itchy because he had the power of getting women pregnant with his look: a popular myth subscribed to by the many coryphaei of bars, church steps, and domino tables; Uncle Itchy who traveled all over the island with a hardware store on his back where he displayed assorted merchandise and in every village and field left a bill for this or that trinket and left a broken heart and left a belly in formation: flatterer, flirter, gadabout: widespread fame: when a tattletale told Mother that the pudding man at the sugar mill and the roadman were sure products of Uncle Itchy, sons with the inherited stamp of restlessness and the trade of coming and going, she replied, honey-toned, resisting third-party talk: I name and claim as nephews the triplets that Itch made in Petra Buchipluma in the Hotel Venus over the post office in Humacao, I name and claim as a niece the child that came cross-eyed out of Petra Buchipluma in the little house in Revuelta del Diablo, I name and claim as nephew the child that Itch made in Petra Buchipluma in the Hotel Euclide. in San Juan and who studied to be a tightrope-walker and is the number one tightrope-walker with the Marco Brothers' Circus. I name and claim as nieces and nephews the nieces and nephews made in bed; the heirs made in the grass, the heirs made standing up at the foot of some ceiba tree are neither here nor there nor there nor here as far as I'm concerned: she shook her hands to show an abstention copied without modesty from the hygienic Pontius Pilate. Hands that Mother shook, hands

FILTHY, SARTRE'S, A notorious memory of her hands: hands still little hands doggedly at work hardening with democratic equity the cousins' peepee places, cousins who didn't return to the Calle del Fuego in the town of Humacao because Mother, scandalized, gasping for breath, overcome by an anxious anxiety, the oxygen cut off in her lungs by the prolonged sessions that the cousins organized under the house, wrote a letter of protest to her sister-in-law Petra Buchipluma in which she said, among other things said: miraculously the girl isn't ruined according to the urine test that Lázara Cuvertier made on her, your three sons have got nasty habits and made her do lewd things under the house that you must remember is built on stilts. I'm sending you Hughie, Louie, and Dewey just the way you sent them to me, without a warning letter, without a penny postcard as a warning. Mother had had her back up ever since she saw Hughie, Louie, and Dewey get off the Experiencia Line jitney as large as life, right at home, without a box of candy, without a little bag of Jacob-stick candy, without a little gift from Padín's, without a little case of little sugar cookies, without a little package of nibble crackers: nothing and she like a regular Penny. Like a regular Pentecostal searching up and down the Calle del Fuego, up and down the Calle de la Ermita, up and down the Calle Font Martelo for a hammock, a hanging bed, a pallet, a folding cot, oh enough of that, and then to dedicate themselves to lewdnesses that if Regino caught them he'd make mincemeat out of them, oh enough of that: to Rosa Berberena in one emission of air. Years later.

IN A SPECIAL sale of trash cans, she found herself, all of a sudden, so that she even got a fright from the great surprise, face to face with one of the cousins, the cousin who'd gone on to be a fireman, a fireman cousin with a great big chest, a fireman cousin who goosed her without a gander, a fireman cousin who greeted her with a question that was an affirmation: say, aren't you the daughter of Aunt Eulalia, the one who kicked me and my brothers out of the house on the Calle del Fuego in Humacao? She, coquettish, pleased with the rubbing and the goosing, answered him, turning her head with open whorish sheen: in the flesh, and she moistened her lips because she calculated, a flash calculation, that with moist lips she'd look more seductive. She answered him as she gave up her place in line to go lean, flowing out, offering herself, against a display of plastic pumpkins: middle of October, Halloween on the horizon. The fireman cousin, a disciple of Jalisco and Jalisco never loses and when it loses it gets excited, also gave up his place in line because the spark that's lighted in cases like that had been lighted; casual, provoking, killing, biting his big mustache a little, he went straight to what he always went to which was his thing: how about that, you were already working me up when you were five. She, amused like someone on a merry-go-round, answered him with interdental ecstasy: you devil, you sneak, you selfish dude, and she got a laughing attack that the fireman cousin calmed with a measured rub on the waist: at five then and thirty now. From the clandestinity of his pocket the fireman cousin tried to calm his fussing whanger. The fireman cousin pushed her with well-dissembled dissembling toward a display of plastic turkeys: Thanksgiving on the horizon. She, moist on the lips, seductive, held him off with a hot whisper that invited more rubbing, contradiction of contradictions all is contradiction: not here, sweetie pie, a plastic turkey as a chastity belt. The fireman cousin promised her a little somersaulting on the following Thursday: what a nice old time we're going to have. A promise that he kept with compound interest at the Hotel Embajador in Cupey Bajo, opposite the dam.

AND LADIES AND gentlemen, friends, that trio of trumpeting trumpets made up of triple terrific trumpets that are Macho Camacho himself in person, Slats Marcano, and Edi Gómez, has got no rival in what's called blowing. Rivalry or competition. And those drums, ladies and gentlemen, friends, no drums like the drums those drums are.

SENATOR VICENTE REINOSA—Vince is a prince and his mind you can't rinse—in order to drive off the shame brought on by the disdain of the schoolgirl who must be round about fifteen when she gets home and washes the pound of makeup down the drain, a shame that wraps around his soul like a strip of crepe paper, whistles, hisses. With a great dose of timidity he whistles, hisses a tune, a little tune, a mock-up, only a mock-up of the rhythm of the guaracha that has taken over the country, drunk in the country, sucked up the country: Macho Camacho's. Almost a reflex, almost a predisposed act, of people oven-baking in the kitchen of intelligence, he can smell me but he can't taste me: quite a ways back and inconsequential, in the penthouse of the brain. But of all buts: Senator Vicente Reinosa—Vince is a prince and respects dissidence—glorifies its arrival on earth, interprets it like a providential sign, glosses it like a messianic step, and unaccepts maintaining the bastardly laziness that the traffic jam brings on in him with the humming of. Thunder, lightning, sparks, eurekas, gollies, wows, heys, shee-eets, fuckitallium; when he becomes aware of his sudden moral fall, when he hastens to slake his thirst with the ordinances of reason, a Job who laments, a Lear who ponders, a Cid at the court of Toledo: who diarrheas, let's say. Hoisted by horror and horrified, he looks to the left hand and to the right hand: no one has heard him sin, seen him sin; praised be his guardian angels: he has five assigned to his

121

privileged position as senator by seniority, no one has heard him sin, seen him sin, because

ALL CHAUFFEURDOM, THE whole passengerial flock, has risen up onto the car roofs in order to find out what the fuck is going on up ahead: a swirl of asking asked by those who have no access to the privileged positions from where one can appreciate what the fuck is going on up ahead. But what do you see, what do you see. A fucking lack of anything clear is what you see. But what do you see, what do you see. You see something like as if the whole avenue were an underground parking garage. But what do you see, what do you see. A sea of scrap iron is what you see. But what do you see, what do you see. You see that the world is going to end caught up in a traffic jam. Prevaricator: the shout and baneful accusation of a Jehovah's Witness who awaits the last judgment sitting in a Dodge Colt: the world will be finalized in fire: his face quartered by death-rattles and biblery and the birth of an off-key canticle aborted immediately: Macho Camacho's guaracha is heating up all antennas. No one saw him sin, heard him sin; in spite of the secretiveness, in spite of not. Shame falls upon the nobility of his head. Macho Camacho's guaracha, its vulgar furor, has tainted him, contaminated him, laid him waste: high or low, a little or a lot, the guaracha: a tiara of vulgarity, a headdress of trash, a banner of the rabble, has alighted on his lips. With a fleeting breeze, of course. But it has alighted: a sin is a sin even though the time might have been used. Sinner, vulgarian, a repetition of Sunday masses, for lack of a hair shirt or penitent's robe, Senator Vicente Reinosa—Vince is a prince and his shame shows blushing tints—raises the sinful eyes of his sinful face to seek an open place, a pleasing resting place, a pilgrim's meadow where he can rest them. In search of the redemptive landscape, greater in size than the tablets advertising Holsum Bread and Kraft Cheese, First National City Bank and Esso Standard Oil Company, he discovers a heroic sign, with italics from the Tablets of Moses, that on high preaches:

MUÑOZ MARÍN IS COMING, REPENT: written with luminous litany spray. MUÑOZ MARÍN IS COMING, REPENT: like a biblical verse arrow-shot into the very guts of his conscience. MUÑOZ MARÍN IS COMING, REPENT: the great shit awaits you like an explosion, brother. MUÑOZ MARÍN IS COMING, REPENT: he's not coming from Sweden like Greta or from Paris like the bébés. MUÑOZ MARÍN IS COMING, REPENT: he's coming from the Via Veneto and the Via Condotti where he was making himself history. MUÑOZ MARÍN IS COMING, REPENT: kneel Puertoricant.

LIKE IT OR not, deny it or not, affirm it or not, Senator Vicente Reinosa—Vince is a prince and his guts never wince —makes an obscure and manual sketch on his forehead, a volatile hieroglyphic that's related to daring tambourine-shaking, like some mummery very much like the sign of the cross, which isn't the sign of the cross but tries to be the sign of the cross, without being it or looking like it: as has been read. Zap. Green Lizard, Pateco the Iridescent, Spirit of the Single Jest: Senator Vicente Reinosa—Vince is a prince and pious as a quince—withdraws, unplugs his eyes from the heroic sign with italics from the Tablets of Moses that preaches on high. In order to banish express genuflections of his insular cant, he accepts the entertainment of the bastardly idleness with an Olympian plunge into the magnificent Olympian asses of some magnificent females who form a pretty pair fucking around on top of a blue Mustang. The fucking around accompanied musically by Macho Camacho's spine-tingling guaracha *Life Is a Phenomenal Thing,* scatterbrained people the little females, dancing about in the hope that two nervy dudes would organize some fun and games for them: my name is Sole, my name is Sole: both of them named Soledad, moaning Afro, rhetorical breasts, eyes that speak a language loaded with intention, my name is Sole, my name is Sole: stepdaughters of Echo.

ONE CHASING THE other, leaping across car tops, lifting up their skirts, giving off sweat at the joints, challenging the sun, playing, dancing, shouting, making flags with their asses as rags: the Soles: this country is too much: don't forget that the late Juancho Gómez asked the church for a dance. An Olympian plunge into the magnificent asses of the magnificent females the Soles: Senator Vicente Reinosa—Vince is a prince and his honesty won't rinse—contemplates and feels a heighdy-ho between his legs: the insomniac animal standing up, he contemplates and hears the dancing chatter of the magnificent females and shoves his thought along: right now, precisely now as I proceed along demented and contented with my task of meeting the mistress of the moment, the mahogany skin of the moment, the copper skin of the moment, exactly now, which is five o'clock sharp, the traffic jam surpasses what is humanly tolerable: there's simply no exit to the Avenida Roosevelt, no exit: existentialist bricks have walled up the exit, bricks from Jean-Paul and Simone, bricks from La Gréco made in the Café Flore, no exit, no exit, over the car tops, in the softness of the seats, in the navel of the heat, in the multiphonic arrangement of the horns, hanging on the doors like monkeys in revolt, drivers and passengers embark upon a Boricuan beating of gums: so much cuchi cuchi, so much holy mother of god, so much opinionizing, so much bad-mouthing, so much when cops direct traffic they really fuck it up, an el or a subway: but the members of the legislature have got the brains of a mosquito: with no offense meant to relations and donations of legislators here present: rolling away at a shirt-sleeve because the sun screws up its own, you ought to know that the sun of Puerto Rico is no pineapple cooler. Blocked all the way to Bayamón: so says a skinny woman whom four bank clerks, four tellers, raise up as a lookout, makes a megaphone with both hands and informs, alarmist: blocked all the way to Bayamón, cuchi cuchi guaracuchi on the car radios, like a majestic guaracuchi overture, like that. Senator Vicente Reinosa—Vince is a prince and his calm makes you wince—states: I'll be late, I'll be late: restates. She, she's the mistress of the moment, won through impatience and fear of attacks and crimes and kidnappings and thefts and shootings and snipers, the daily bill of fare in the country, she'll leave, she's quite capable of leaving while I'm caught in the need of coming. With his wife he already knows:

ALL FRECKLES AND white, all mysterious refusal, all careful and slow and soft and finish and when are you going to finish and let me say a God Save You Queen and Mother, let me say a Hail Mary and let me say an Our Father or she pretends to be asleep or she pretends not to understand or she demands a tomblike silence from me because she's in the red tape of transcendental meditation and imposes twin beds so that in the crossing of that glacial abyss erotic dispositions will die: a double bed is natural: he notices the rub of a leg, the dropping of a hand: nothing doing, don't insist, I don't, you don't what, I don't, you make me nervous, smeared with Pond's cream, smeared with Eterna 27, smeared with Second Début, masked with a mask of, thick wool socks because I'm cold or the beginnings of arthritis, a netting with little lead weights in the hem: mosquitoes, roaches, insects: but you're delirious, but I'm a lady, good night: she goes to sleep or pretends that she goes to sleep: annoyed, rejected, I go to the refrigerator, I click the refrigerator door, I drink a glass of milk, I eat a piece of Sara Lee cake, no. I'm not going to wake up the maid, I'm not a swine, I'm a gentleman: to dare or not to dare, to dare or not to dare: Hamlet with the skull, me with the piece of Sara Lee cake, to dare or not to: Testiviton, a promise at twelve o'clock at night: to stop taking Testiviton or to take it every four days. Fine and refined, a gentleman and gentlemanly.

CHANGING THE SUBJECT, what a change with his mistress in exchange for a financial patronage guaranteed by the coffers of the country, what an ardent response to his dynamic Eros, what a hot reception for his unsuspected requests: what a talent for pirouettes: a pirouette on the bed, a pirouette on the armchair, a pirouette on the floor, a pirouette at the edge of the washbowl, a pirouette in the bathtub: most worthy forerunners of the *Last Tango in Paris:* the medicine chest chock full of sponges, the refrigerator chock full of bars of Blue Bonnet butter: what a startling versatility for the creation and maintenance of unlikely steps: as long as the lover is a black or mulatto woman. Black or mulatto: the worst-kept secret of the Senate or the August Parliamentary Palace at Puerta de Tierra: in the endless coffee breaks, in the roll calls, in the Whiskery that is the office of the weighty and respected Senator Guzmán, at banquets, the blowhard and sempiternal Senator Guzmán, peer of a pair of motels, leader of the bosses, leader of the workers, a sonneteer in telluric alexandrines, would banter: Vince the Slavetrader, Vince the Housemaider: muffled coughs from Senators Felipe Bengocosta and Raimundo Velázquez, permanent guests at hotels and cabarets where their station paid the ration of liquored greetings. Slavetrader, halfbreeder, housemaider. And there's that fucking guaracha: but on these radio discos there aren't any other records: popularity, friend, popul.

INTERRUPTION OF THE hit parade on the number one station of Antillean radio in order to present to hysterical and historical annals an extra that's extra extra: a bomb at the University. Bomb explodes at the University of Puerto Rico. Bomb explodes at the Faculty of Social Sciences at the University of Puerto Rico. Bomb explodes at the Ramón Emeterio Betances Faculty of Social Sciences at the University of Puerto Rico. The effects of the bomb have not been determined but officials of the Criminal Investigation Division, officials of the FBI, officials of the Riot Police have cordoned off the complex of buildings that holds, among others, the Faculty of: interruption to beg a thousand pardons for the previous interruption, an interruption of the ecstasy of the moment, the ecstasy plows through the quadrant, an ecstasy that reminds us that life is a phenomenal thing. Bela Lugosi, Frankenstein, The Creature from the Black Lagoon.

AND THE ECSTASY of the moment, ladies and gentlemen, friends, pouring out of the acumen of Macho Camacho to impose itself on the imposition of the wailing duo of Sandro and Raphael, on the Queen of Latin Song Lucecita, over and above the fabled Tom Jones, leaving Chucho Avellanet an orphan, anyone who sings just for singing stays at the end of the line, Serrat takes a beating, not even the great Danny Rivera can escape, all liquidated by the sweeping drive of Macho Camacho, who's like the priest or pastor or preacher of the thing.

GRACIELA THUMBS THROUGH the latest *Time:* People have got to know whether or not their President is a crook. Well, I'm not a crook. Graciela skips over the pages of international news in *Time:* Allende or death in cold blood. Graciela skips over the pages of literary criticism in *Time:* Vonnegut's *Breakfast of Champions.* Graciela turns over with horror and disgust some shots of napalmized Vietnam reproduced in *Time* because she can't tolerate even a minute of anguish: nothing painful, nothing mournful, nothing miserable, nothing sad: I wasn't born for that: it's good not being born to look at children fried to a crisp by flamethrowers and fright, people who are lucky, damn it but it's good. Graciela stops fas-ci-na-ted, en-chan-ted, be-wit-ched, looking at the fascinating, enchanting, bewitching photograph of Liz and Richard's house in Puerto Vallaita published as a graphic supplement of *Time.* Typical and topical: a nostalgic mansion from the days of Don Porfirio with Mauser holes by a battalion of the hosts of Victoriano Huerta, bougainvillaea and prickly-pear cactus limbs in whose skeletal shade peasant women make tortillas, tortillas cooked in a clay dish as red as the earth from which it was made, menacing petroglyphs of Tlaloc and Quetzalcoatl resting on the balcony: *Time* or a novel by Carlos Fuentes? On a corner there is a rusty handorgan with a musical roll of *Adelita.* A hundred sighs later, nauseated from the swaying of her thoughts, her head besieged by a mortification alien to dandruff and hemipterous insects, Graciela turns another page and. Oh. Oh. Oh. Oh; the Donald Duck tantrum. A little spider suspended from its thread with all its dots is not as much in suspense, oh, oh, oh, more in suspense than a piece of paper with a series of suspended dots:

ONCE UPON A time there was a little princess named Jacqueline who married the King of Scorpion Island. The King of Scorpion Island was a comrade of Midas and had gold eyes and had a gold nose and had a gold mouth and had a gold chest and had a gold navel and the head of his prick was not gold but was filled with gold. Graciela edits out unedited orgasms, Graciela edits out uterine heat waves, Graciela edits out mucous secretions: Princess Jacqueline dressed to ride a wild boar, Princess Jacqueline dressed to eat French fries, Princess Jacqueline dressed to give alms to the poor, Princess Jacqueline dressed to call Baroness Marie-Hélène Rothschild on the telephone. There are things that because they are such things are not to be told: the pins of painful pleasure prick and prick and prick the pride of Graciela Alcántara y López de Montefrío. Graciela Alcántara y López de Montefrío, pricked and pricked and pricked by the painful pleasure of the pins of pleasure, throws *Time* into the air, flings *Time* into the air, hurls *Time* into the air, shrieks with pain, shrieks with resentment, shrieks with shrieking: that's living, that's living, that's living, Graciela Alcántara y López de Montefrío gives leaps like a monkey in heat or monkeyed leaps, gives leaps like a gorilla in heat or gorillaed leaps, that's living, that's living, that's living. In short: her pride turns to confetti.

THE RECEPTIONIST: THE fainting spell: but she was faking crazy, putting on a crazy act. The Nurse and Receptionist, confused and surprised by the craziness of the quiet little crazy woman, faking crazy, putting on a crazy act, doesn't realize that she's raising the volume on the transistor until it reaches the mark that indicates that the volume won't go any higher: tautological. Who doesn't know: Macho Camacho's guaracha inflames the plastic-covered diplomas that hang on the wall as an accreditation of Doctor Severo Severino's capacity to confront succulent emotions; inflamed by the demisemiquavers and the hemidemisemiquavers of Macho Camacho's guaracha, the shiny certificate that certifies that Doctor Severo Severino attended and passed the course in *How to Win Friends and Influence People* offered by the Dale Carnegie Institute glows; inflamed by the quavers and semiquavers of Macho Camacho's guaracha the shiny certificate that certifies that Doctor Severo Severino attended and passed the course in *How to Be Happy in Seven Days* glows. Naturally: the pandemonium alerts Doctor Severo Severino who was playing a game of Monopoly with a landowner's wife who, besides possessing a lot of land, possessed a depressive mania that was alleviated by table games: parcheesi, Monopoly, hearts, blackjack: the pandemonium and the Nurse and Receptionist and the violation of the door to the study where succulent emotions are distilled and: Doctor, Miss Hoity-Toity has flipped. Doctor

Severo Severino: how many times have I told you about language and the way you use it and. The Nurse and Receptionist: Doctor, the flat-chested white woman has blown her stack. Come and look, come and see: the manic-depressive wife of the landowner goes out a window and from the sidewalk demands the return of her hotels. Doctor Severo Severino tosses the hotels out the window and she hastens to put them away in her purse. The manic-depressive wife of the landowner demands the houses on Boardwalk, the houses on Madison Avenue. Doctor Severo Severino tosses the houses out the window. The manic-depressive wife of the landowner demands all the money. Doctor Severo Severino tosses paper money valued at fifty thousand dollars out the window and runs and flies and flies and runs with his best plastic smile to give proper attention to Graciela Alcántara y López de Montefrío. Graciela Alcántara y López de Montefrío cuts off her orangutanic leap number one hundred twelve to ask: Doctor, why Liz and not me? why Jacqueline and not me? If you can't answer those questions you're going to put me on suicide balcony. The Nurse and Receptionist: chocolate ice cream is very good for the nerves and with pineapple syrup it's even better: a whisper. The Nurse and Receptionist: why would the Doctor want to put out my eyes?

LET'S GO INTO the office, beautiful woman, well-dressed woman, well-shod woman, well-made-up woman, woman taken by the waist, Graciela Alcántara y López de Montefrío's head rests on Doctor Severo Severino's shoulder, an unscrupulous person might suspect that the second act of

Swan Lake is starting: Siegfried and Odette heading for the wings to begin the great pas de deux. The tape recorder, the notebook, a relaxation so fabricated that it falls into tension, sighs, a cough, a witticism funny I was thinking about you yesterday, a coquetry, your nerves are elegant nerves, a don't laugh at me because the laughter of humanity hurts me, an I'm not laughing at you, an I'm laughing with you, a life is so cruel, a one doesn't want life to be so cruel and: after a sigh that recapitulates a hundred of them, her eyes browse along the beam and the ice goes crack: in February. From her charming kidskin purse, most delicate and dear, Graciela extracts the cigarette case of fine gold charged at William Cobb, Jewelers. Graciela extracts from the cigarette case the cigarette that she lights at the unfiltered end, something else harmful.

DOCTOR, IT ISN'T really a question of nerves. I'm a balanced woman, in charge of every one of my acts, acts over which I exercise enviable control and manipulation, invigorated by my noonday mass at the Cathedral, my donation of old clothes to the poor, the little envelope with the monthly dollars that I send for the charitable work of the Old People's Home. The ice goes crack and breaks: the thing started in February. Sometimes, not often, it didn't go beyond an upset manifested by a sudden loss of breath, a quick chill, or a peculiar way of dealing with the simplest situations: weak coffee or strong coffee or coffee neither weak nor strong or hot coffee or cold coffee or coffee that doesn't taste like coffee or coffee that tastes like wood or coffee that tastes like funeral flowers or coffee that tastes like lettuce. Crazy, annoyed, terrified, I thought about an autumn pregnancy.

THE WORD AUTUMN mortgages her memory with layer cakes crested with leaping cupids and little meringue figures of Philemon and Baucis with raisin eyes and candy buttons. Quite false, the word autumn brings her long memories of black-and-white movies with the red-headed comedienne who was Liza Minnelli's mother-in-law, no not Bette Davis's. Bette Davis's yes, Bette Davis pregnant by Gary Cooper or pregnant by Bogart, Bette Davis pregnant by Clark Gable and dressed in serge frocks and a line that went around the corner to the Cine Riviera and bags of popcorn and. A lie. The word autumn plagues her with moving memories, pitiful memories of a soap opera with the main role played by the deeply tragic Madeline Willemsen, the great Madeline Willemsen destroyed, episode after episode, by the absolute perversity of a swinish engineer who pawns the precious pearl necklace given her by an Austrian count, an Austrian count who was no such Austrian count but was an apache from the lower depths of Paris, Telemundo presents the deeply tragic Madeline Willemsen and, False, false, false, amnesiac, forgetful, the star of the series was the great Lucy Boscana, Telemundo presents the outstanding leading lady Lucy Boscana and Boscana would appear on screen during the whole story with a string of pearls with which she hanged herself in the last episode after discovering, a naturalistic scene, that she was crippled from birth. The story was called *Pearls of Autumn*, the story was called *The Autumn of*

the Pearls, the story was called *Pearls of My Autumn,* Telemundo presents.

AFTER THAT CAME the vomiting, very much worse:
the feeling of an imminent vomiting attack that had second
thoughts after it had already entered the garden of the esopha-
gus, after it had already embittered the intestines, after it had
already embittered the periphery of the tonsils. In the name of
God and those who abide with Him: a late pregnancy is impossible in spite of the ramblings just told. No. Besides, her husband and she haven't. For a long, long time. Her husband all
wrapped up in political activity. Besides, my son is, is, is. I'm
so bad at dates. Besides, I'm not the kind of lady who considers
that important. With moral repugnance she pronounces the
pronoun and ties it up with knots of sacred disgust. I'm too
much of a lady and as a lady I treat *that* with its quota of
disgust, I feel relieved when my husband goes to sleep without
any hint of the least bit of interest in *that.* Besides, I love him,
there's no doubt that I love him because he's my husband and
God has commanded us to love our husbands and I love God
very much. But it's one thing with a violin and something else
with a guitar. *That* always seemed cheap to me. Not cheap.
Low. Not low. Base. Not base. Vile. Vile and the voices that
rule naked blood come from hell, *that,* a sin, ugh: like stepping
in shit, an urge to spit from so much disgust.

SHE DOESN'T SPIT because in Switzerland snowy and
pure she learned not to spit. Because in Switzerland snowy and

pure people don't spit, in this blessed Puerto Rico they do: a reflection that pricks her at certain moments every day: in this country they spit a lot, in this country they spit too much, in this country they spit all over the place, in this country they spit in a thousand different ways, rich and poor, men and women, at all hours, at unexpected moments, in the air-conditioned mall of the Plaza Las Américas she sees it, in the canopied café of Las Nereidas she sees it: spitting: a déclassé habit of a déclassé country: Isabella and Ferdinand never should have.

AND LADIES AND gentlemen, friends, how well the leather skins are punished, whipped, tortured by that skillful attacker named Corino Alonso. He's called the criminal of the bongó, the baby of the dried skin, the daddy of the leather, the baby-spanker.

"BAH," ARGUES THE Old Man whose Mistress The Mother was, hands wheeling in the air, arms. "Tut," argued The Old Man whose Mistress The Mother was, putting ice into the ice bucket. "Nonsense, legends beyond all scientific consideration," argued The Old Man whose Mistress The Mother was, fools, foolishness, a wild conception of reality: gesticulating. "The foolish primitivism of people who oppose reason with superstition," argued The Old Man whose Mistress The Mother was, arranging three ices cubes in a tall glass, a tall highball glass with contrived Egyptian sketches of heroes and tombs. "Exposure to the sun's rays is absolutely beneficial for the skin exposed," argued The Old Man whose Mistress The Mother was, his great toe opening a pedestrian path along the nipple of The Mother who was The Old Man's Mistress. "Sun baths are among the most ancient forms of therapy," argued The Old Man whose Mistress The Mother was, placing the glass with the highball on the small table placed at the end of the sofa with an aim to have highball glasses placed there, the great toe of his left foot opening a pedestrian path along the right nipple of The Mother who was The Old Man's Mistress. "In France before the Republic sun baths were used as part of the treatment for benign lunatics," argued The Old Man whose Mistress The Mother was, clasping the waist of The Mother who was The Old Man's Mistress, clasping it with his feet, playing at tightening, enjoying the seasick sway of the

feet, the tickling. "Benign lunatic is the psychic category to which The Kid belongs," argued The Old Man whose Mistress The Mother was, kneeling down, seeding the thighs with strokes and breathing, seeding the thighs, separating them: a sumptuous banquet in the sacred zone.

THE MOTHER OBEYS. The Mother, of course, obeys. The Mother is obedient. The Mother leaves The Kid in the little park on the Calle Juan Pablo Duarte. The Mother leaves The Kid lying in a corner of the little park on the Calle Juan Pablo Duarte. The Mother leaves The Kid lying, sunning, in a corner of the little park on the Calle Juan Pablo Duarte because The Kid is a lump. That's all she needed: The Mother doesn't disappear just like that as if she were any little everyday mother. None of that, nothing, nothing of that. The Mother knows a lot of mothers' songs, The Mother knows a lot of mothers' pasodobles, The Mother knows a lot of mothers' tangos. The Mother's seen a lot of Mexican movies. The Mother is a steady customer of the Cine Matienzo, the Cine New President. The Mother fondles The Kid: Mama, Mama, Mama, I say, kiss me, kiss me, every day: Sara García, Libertad Lamarque, Mona Marti, Amparo Rivelles. The Mother dandles him. The Mother swears that God Almighty will reward him if he behaves himself, that God Almighty will love him very much if he behaves himself, and other pious pieces of stupidity that bounce off the face that shows no sorrow, joy, or human feeling.

UNDER A SUN irritated by its own candescence, did rubicund Apollo settle in spite of himself on a city called San

Juan?, rubicund Apollo, wonderworker of close-up suns?, rubicund Apollo with the combustion of another day of ours?, the mockery shines just as bright: games of taunts, games of dirty digs with both mouth and sticks acted out through a stormy afternoon: a cocktail of blues and clouds leaping scrub and trash and passing over a two-story house and dodging dogs that pass: snorting and unhealthy happiness when a dry stick makes its entry into his lobe and The Kid curls up into a gongolí worm, pasteurized milk of human nastiness and boiling in twenty eyes open to all evil, curdled milk whipped with howls: crackling of homicidal intent from the children who pull on The Kid's little boneless tuna arms. Until the urge to break him is broken and frustrated; mewing of enjoyed villainy from the left-out children who, stationed on a fountain, contemplate the enjoyment and enjoy it. And they wait: stepchildren of the Old West with broad-brimmed hats, broad brims in the tradition of Gene Autry, silver cartridge belts in the tradition of Hopalong Cassidy, mewing of enjoyed villainy from the pistols and revolvers piled up in the arsenal tradition of Capone, Dillinger, and Bonnie and Clyde, Bonnie and Clyde brought back to life in the ballad stitched on a shirt:

> Some day we will go down together
> And they will bury us side by side.
>> To a few it means grief,
>> To the law it's relief,
> But it's death to Bonnie and Clyde.

Mewing of enjoyed villainy from a Barbie doll sitting ominously on the fountain's highest perch: bleating enriched by the tantrums of the children who wet their fingers in the drool, drooly fingers wiped on denim or the halter of a jumper, rather pretty, all in Scotch plaid; croaking of competitive vileness, hoots with the hopscotch game, squawks with the everybody spit on him: all dismounted and leaped down from the fountain and from the swings and from a carob tree and that demented Amazonia that ten healthy children stir up: they're all chubby wild boars, sturdy wolf cubs, wild colts, agile fighting cockerels, magnificent unfelinated jimmies and juniors and johnnies, obstinate tyro rogues, blond projections of mafiosi and free-enterprisers: a statue of saliva is what they put together, twisted slightly and made of saliva.

SHE WAS SCRATCHING her skirt, she was pinched by a pleat: an impression communicated by the enthusiasm or desperation with which she scratched her skirt, her skin not perturbed, the unperturbed skin of Doña Chon. Doña Chon, high priestess of rice and beans, unconquered maker of stuffed potatoes, repository of the secret of the most delicious codfish poached with egg in the world, mater et magistra of chicken broth, holy hand for pumpkin pancakes, was stirring a tureen of tripe that would give the taste of the century to the masons on strike. "I thought the ones on strike were the airport drivers," said The Mother, brushing away at the head that held the blond wig, precariously seated on a folding chair that she'd dragged over from her house, the house where she slept. Because her day-to-day life was spent at Doña Chon's, the houses opposite each other, barely fifty feet between one door and the other, the backyard was water: the mangrove swamp. "The airport drivers, the drivers for the Blanca Tirado fleet, the blouse-makers on the Calle Guano, the municipal employees, the boys who sell hamburgers at the entrance to the Llorens housing project," said Doña Chon, the smoke eating at her eyes. "Half the country on strike and the other half getting ready," said Doña Chon, her eyes eaten by the smoke. "First there's the firemen's strike, then there's the teachers' strike," said Doña Chon: prophetic. "And the firemen go all the way," said The Mother: the experience of a lot of flying time. "Then there's the utility strike," said Doña Chon. "I used to open the refrigerator from far off because the ice chills me," said Doña Chon. "At least the loonies' strike is over," said Doña Chon. Doña Chon was giving witchlike stirs to the tripe and opening her hand from a considerable and suspicious height was dropping coriander leaves into the boiling dish and muttering uncertain vowels directed at Our Tasty Lady of Coriander. "The loonies' strike didn't last long," said The Mother, brushing away at the head that held the black wig. Doña Chon, the winning ace in her hand, the tureen of tripe as a bar to support an arabesque of tight extension: because they were federal loonies, m'girl, people turned crazy in Korea and Vietnam. "Here, what's federal is tricky, tricky, tricky," said Doña Chon, spoken with a shout because in the café called The Sin of Being Poor Macho Camacho's guaracha was imposing a regime of absolutism. The Mother, brushing away at the head that held the red wig, sighingly: oh mother!:

"CURDS AND BLOOD sausage and little green bananas for starters," said Doña Chon. "Platters of fried pieces of codfish to finish the openers," said Doña Chon. "The tripe and the load of garlic bread to lay in front of the open stomach," said Doña Chon. "The pot of corn and coconut and the tray of milk candy to start the end," said Doña Chon. "Pots of coffee to end it once and for all," said Doña Chon: escorted by eight stoves on which frying-pans, lard, and pots crackled. "You are what you eat," said Doña Chon. Doña Chon was putting the spoon into the deep little pot that she loved. Doña Chon was eating like an open sore. "It's one thing to eat and something else to feel the meal settling down at the bottom of your stomach," said Doña Chon. Doña Chon, pray for us fatties now and at the hour of slimming diets by Weight Watchers. "My thing is to eat and to ball," said The Mother, wiping off the remains of the tripe on the sleeve of her blouse, satisfied as an old dog. "My thing is to eat until I shit," said The Mother, expansive and oozing confidence, sucking away on a pig's foot. Severe, perturbed, Doña Chon: unwanted things are not spoken at table. The Mother, flustered, her tail between her legs, hides behind the pig's foot, in a mangled English tongue, in shrapnel English: excuse me. The Mother, fixing things up, smoothing things over, making things happy: Doña Chon, if you'll take The Kid for me this afternoon I'll give you a little something and the little something will help you pay Tutú's lawyer. "Tutú," sighed Doña Chon. Doña Chon put away the deep little pot she loved. Doña Chon let go of the spoon. Doña Chon returned a rebellious tangle of hair to the entanglement. "Tutú," repeated Doña Chon, an arm over her eyes, as if her heartstrings had become untied, as if her face were waiting for the sawdust filling that would fill it, a great doll torn asunder, a decunted doll for the rest of the afternoon, saddened by the name that had been spoken. A fondled and possible metaphor: like mist that could be cut with a knife. The Mother returned the pig's foot to one side of the plate where other little bones were building a community.

"*LIFE IS A* bundle of dirty clothes," said Doña Chon: defining, a leaf of sadness hanging from her look. "Life is like a bundle of dirty clothes but it's a bundle of problems," said Doña Chon: academic and judicious in her tone. "Men don't realize that life is a bundle of dirty clothes but one made up of problems," said Doña Chon: discriminating. "Doña Chon, you're the kind of person who could do a good job at writing guarachas," said The Mother: dreaming, respectful like the prostitute. Doña Chon: I'm an honest homebody: answered in a neutral tonality impossible to interpret. "A man doesn't even know this much," she held the tips of her thumb and forefinger together, "about what pain is," said Doña Chon, argumentative. "No man can ever give birth," said Doña Chon, bombastic in the formulation of the historic assertion. "Men are missing the little screw in the push-ahead part that's a little screw that a woman has in her part," said Doña Chon: gynecologist. "The day a man wants to know what it's like to give birth, let him try shitting out a pumpkin," said The Mother: euphoric, a kindergarten in her ovaries, fanfare with the tubas of Fallopius.

AND IT ALL went wild, ladies and gentlemen, friends. Because bring on your records and more records, interviews in entertainment magazines, an invitation to represent our little island at the Caribbean fun festival and the end-all of all end-alls: an invitation to play at Loíza Aldea on the selfsame day of the Apostle Saint James and expose himself to the demanding and wise judgment of crab-fishing blacks, masters of what taste is really all about.

BENNY SAYS AT noon: my beautiful Ferrari and composes an acrostic by way of greeting with letters from some Campbell's soup. Benny spends the whole afternoon driving around in his Ferrari, from San Juan to Caguas, from Caguas to San Juan, from Cataño to Dorado, from Dorado to Cataño. Benny doesn't drive from Barrio Obrero to Quince because Barrio Obrero to Quince is a stone's throw. I mean Papi I'll go nuts if I can't jam down the accelerator, if I can't shift gears until they say: you've just made the perfect shift. At night after a warm shower and saudade for the Ferrari: it's probably thinking about me just the way I'm thinking about it, after the bye-bye he bids the carport where the Ferrari is alone and waiting, Benny heads for his room, after walking around the Ferrari four times, giving it looks that could be translated as have a good night's sleep, looks that are sighs, honey-sweet with tender words, cooing, and assorted whorey terms. At night, after the above-mentioned ritual, Benny gets into bed, pulls up the covers, and says: ugly, Catholic, and sentimental: Our Ferrari which art in the carport, hallowed be Thy Name, I mean thy kingdom of motor and chassis. And man, forgive us the sin of driving you like you were a tortoise, amen. Amen and turning his hulk to face the wall with a mirror where the polychrome, polyfaceted, polyphonic, polyform, polypetaled, polyvalent body of his Ferrari stands out. Amen and turning

his hulk on its back and impatient exhalations because night
has interposed itself between him and the Ferrari. Amen and
turning his hulk toward the dresser, toward the wall again,
toward the ceiling light again, bothered by dumb insomnia,
amen and

THE HAND THAT plays with the soft nakedness of his
body, a nakedness attacked by the easy access spaced out between buttons, a hand that struts across the vacant lot he has
between his paps, a hand that winds among the thin surplus
folds about his waist, kneading and caressing and peekaboo
because he won't let the hand burst onto the altar or touch or
stroke the officiant. Kneading and caressing and a hand that
suddenly invades his pubescence: a beneficial buzzing that
extends down to the balls, the hand that gives sensation attends
the birth of a delight as yet fragmented. A fragmented delight
observed in the half-hardness of the officiant. An officiant that
now rises and falls like a drunkard, rises and falls like a drunkard, rises and stretches and stands stiff as a bobbin: the com-
pleted erection. Benny, carried away by meat-beating fantasies,
overcome by a killing deviltry, seeks the copy of *El Mundo* that
collaborates in these chores. Benny flies to the washbowl because jerking off with a wet hand is for revolutionaries and
other shitheads. Benny gives himself over to an invocatory
swoon, his hand attains the automotive speed denied the Ferrari: Ferrari all chrome, Ferrari all wax, Ferrari all nickel, Ferrari all intercepted by Benny's confused kisses, Ferrari pierced,
Ferrari penetrated by Benny's desire, the gas tank torn by
Benny's desire, by Benny's officiant, Ferrari gorged by Benny's

semen. AAAAH the cry made within and Benny's ascension to a celebration without equal: one of the great comings of the century. The hand exhausted by the mileage covered for pleasure, the exhausted hand gripping the officiant that falls and rises like a drunkard, falls and rises, falls and the convulsion and the throbbing and a sleep that cloaks and beckons him.

I MEAN THAT the important thing is for today's youth to have a voice, today's youth are needing ears, us young people have got stuff to say, ideas about how life ought to be set up that young people have got hidden away in their brains. I mean us young people have got a great future in what's coming. I mean for example it isn't good for every kid of eighteen not to have his wheels. I mean I'm not saying he should have a Ferrari which would only be right since he's never going to be eighteen again which is one of the problems that really is a problem. I mean speaking realistically that he should have his Ford, should have his Toyota, should have his Datsun, should have his Cortina, should have his Cougar, should have his Rambler, should have his Chevvy, should have his Comet, should have his Renault: the important thing is for him to have his car or his jalopy or his heap or his shell on four wheels. I mean that rebellion or rage or anger are only natural because no teen-ager can get along without the friendship of his car or his jalopy or his heap or his wheels. I mean us young people are younger than old people. I mean if some arrangement could be made where old people could be as young as young people the world would be painted different: an incisive point of view that reveals Benny's acumen, a Solomonic point of view, let us have no doubts that its attainment and adoption would shake the very foundations of gerontological pharmacopeia, would make the word aging an anachronism, would screw Max Factor and Clairol's creamy commerce, would reduce Beauvoir's latest book to the interest of antediluvian bibliophiles. The author: Benny, please recapitulate. I mean that if old people: the broken-record technique, a bonus for critics and reviewers.

BENNY SOLILOQUIZES BREATHLESSLY, although he's no Belmondo, he soliloquizes, pollparrotizes: in the same way as if he were a character with an exaggerated, contradictory, ambiguous inner life, negation after affirmation. Benny, you've heard him, you've seen him, is a one-dimensional character: there are no links with Emma or Charles, nor are there any with the most simple-minded Buendía, he's no Lazarillo, no Ana Ozores, much less a Goriot or a Sorel, not a hair of Robert Jordan, impossible for him to be an Usmail or a Pirulo. One-dimensional Benny lives and dies for the justification of his sloth, a sloth that is idleness raised to the third power. An only child; the family takes pleasure in gratifying his sustained sloth: a family that pampers, a family that struts, a well-heeled family. The family, father and mother, avoids calling it sloth. The family, father and mother, speaks of conflicts that belong to the conflictive age, of a stumble in the process of adaptation, of the hostility of the environment, of the rise of a repugnant egalitarianism, the actions of a naughty boy, the naughty behavior of a boy thing, harmful friends. The family fosters his laziness in order to draw him away from activities because of which only their personal connections with the judicial and legislative branches have kept him out of jail or a hard time: a family with a firm grip on the handle of the pot, the handle above all. The cliques, of course, the cliques: cliques is what the family calls the rest of humanity that shares the planet Earth with Benny; one mustn't forget that, among other things, Benny is an Earthling. Cliques with which he planned, back in February, the plot chronicled here, a plot that didn't go beyond the limits of the family circle: are we or are we not the government, are we or are we not one of the leading families in the country, are we or are we not the bearers of a first-class name, are we or are we not members of high society. On the Reinosa side you can go back to the line of Juana la Beltraneja, on the Alcántara side you can go back to the line of Guzmán el Bueno: an act of fuming faith on the part of Papi Papikins.

THE PLOT WAS plotted by Bonny, an intimate friend of Benny. The conjoiners were conjoined by no less than Willy and Billy. Willy was a friend of Benny, Billy was a friend of Bonny. Great friends, in short, Benny, Bonny, Willy, and Billy. Benny, Bonny, Willy, and Billy were, besides Benny, Bonny, Willy, and Billy, the lifetime overseers of the rites of initiation into a fraternity that was, besides being a fraternity of swimming pools and drinking bouts, a tabernacle of manly idiocy: renowned for their Grecian profiles or noses exempt from flatness, the sons of fathers whose fathers were the founders of authority, they spent the fat part of their thin lives in the montage and choreography of blue blazers where candidates demonstrated the firmness of their character and will through rigorous tests such as the placing of the buttocked passage on a cake of ice, gargling with pristine urine, sack races, and, of course: the investigation of the immediate and remote past of the neophytes: if you're black, get back.

PLOTTING THE PLOT was Bonny, the intimate friend of Benny: taking advantage of the shades of night, taking advantage of the indifference of the police in order to reduce to rubble, to ashes, or to reduce to cinders the offices of the separatists, antisocial scum, the offices and workshops where they print and do their presswork, poisoning nordophilic sentiment. Explosives, a dynamite charge, a right-wing pharmacy, a clock, gorging in a pizzeria. And how well they did their thing! And how laughter tightened their cheeks! And how they jeered and enjoyed and partied when the press, ooh-la-la, in a small item placed on the obituary page, printed a few lines saying that the arsonists left no traces by means of which the plot could be investigated: *life is a phenomenal thing:* a line from the guaracha of the hour.

A SECOND DANGEROUS deed and attributed to the evil cliques, in spite of the well-kept secret: the plot was plotted by Benny: a screw in quadruplicate, a screw in celebration of the success of the bombing, a screw in which the one screwed would be a big old whore of great fame because she played pool and had a hairy mole on her breast and on her thighs of hambone thickness displayed the artistic tattoo of a ship sinking between two waves. La Metafísica by name. Outrageous Metafísica, insolent Metafísica who, filthy and bedraggled and topsergeantly, lifted weights on Saturdays. A whore who kept in her room a beam that had the weight of Muhammad Ali, Esteban de Jesús, and George Foreman, and kept in her room a yellow fighting cock she was training to fight in the Good Luck cockpit in the city of Fajardo. A valiant whore who collected for her tricks in advance and would repeat, "A musician plays better when he's paid up front." A defiant whore who with fearless and amazing trust kept the money she earned in a cigar box. In open view of everybody: whether cherry boys, whether experienced studs, whether the Three Wise Men: if anyone so much as looks at my loot I'll break his arm or bust his neck. That's how she thundered. And like a stevedore, she would rub her biceps. One by one the four celebrants did their thing, without any fun because the fun was in the surprise. No sooner had Bonny climbed onto the hambone-thick thighs, no sooner had his chicken thighs run up against the ship sinking between two waves, than Benny burst into the room and shouted a terrible command of *dismount.* As soon as Bonny had dismounted, recounted later amidst attacks of laughter, into La Metafísica's shocked place they stuck a sparkler which would convert her instantaneously into an enlightened whore. She raged, roared, spat on their memory and that of their mothers, grandmothers, sisters, and other female kin to whom she wished a fearsome fate. La Metafísica, who serviced judges and bailiffs, went to court and demanded justice for herself and indemnification for the business that she conducted between her legs. The case was unheard by the judge at the hearing, and from then on the friendship of the four horsemen of the apocalypse fell apart or went into retreat: the counsel of the council of fathers brought together to examine the gravity of the matter: they were to be separated, in case one of them snitched, in case one of them squealed. And to keep them company in their punishment: a car for each.

AND LADIES AND gentlemen, friends, feel in your flesh what's in your flesh, that is, the meatball we make human as we make ourselves human, feel the jab of the guaracha. Because, ladies and gentlemen, friends, just close your eyes a little and when you look again you'll roar with delight at the heights reached by this opera in guaracha time that is Macho Camacho's guaracha.

THE FIREMAN COUSIN, a disciple of Jalisco and Jalisco never loses and when it loses it gets excited, also gave up his place in line because the spark that's lighted in cases like that had been lighted; casual, provoking, killing, biting his big mustache a little, he went straight to what he always went to which was his thing. With a voice of give me what's mine, Valentine, he gave out with what's given out here: how about that, you were already working me up when you were five. He had the smell of a pimp. She, amused like someone on a merry-go-round, answered him with interdental ecstasy: you devil, you sneak, you selfish dude. And she got a laughing attack that the fireman cousin calmed with a measured rub on the waist: at five then and thirty now. From the clandestinity of his pocket, the fireman cousin tried to calm his fussing whanger. The fireman cousin pushed her without dissembling up against a display of plastic turkeys: Thanksgiving on the horizon. She, moist on the lips, seductive, held him off with a hot whisper that invited more rubbing, contradiction of contradictions all is contradiction: not here, sweetie pie, a plastic turkey as a chastity belt. The fireman cousin promised her a little somersaulting on the following Thursday: what a nice old time we'll have. A promise that he kept, with compound interest, at the Hotel Embajador in Cupey Bajo, opposite the dam. She let her memory linger and let the sip of cubalibre linger in her mouth and in her mouth she felt the ghost of a different tongue, of different tongues, tongue and rum in a both at the same time, another cubalibre please: to herself.

YOU DOWN THEM to drown: The Old Man will declare when he arrives, does he declare it out of a moral imperative or out of stinginess? No one knows because he's an autonomous character, he will, though, kiss her on the cheek as if she were his wife: making fun of the halfbreed or the sublimation or the entry of his sly tricks, the ostrich-skin briefcase deposited on the reclining chair, two fingers of rum left in the quart. You down them and you drown: a repetition or a variation on a theme by Ravel or a characteristic of style to be commented on in a doctoral thesis: anaphora. The Old Man will observe the adventure in the disarray: in the ashtray, next to a smoking butt, lies an empty sausage can; under the sofa one can deduce the snout of a shoe, a bra hangs from the knob of the front door; newsreel of an intimacy where her bare nakedness resides, her nipples daubed with honey as a plaything in their play, he will put his jacket on one hanger and his pants on another so as not to wrinkle them, no, enunciated, caught and released like the ball in basketball, like mouthfuls of a drama, like a one-act play for only two actors, just like Tennessee Williams' last play, but in *Outcry* they were brother and sister, like brother and sister we'll be holding hands, he'll kiss me on the cheek as if I were his wife and with the other hand he'll hold me around the waist, return a stray lock to the bright red wig, when The Old Man comes.

TO A LITTLE WATCH where two fake rubies reside that her husband had sent her from the north: to inveigle her, to butter her up so she wouldn't be taken by surprise. She probably knew: they'd tattled to her that her husband was living in a basement apartment with a Chicano woman but for her everything was plink. Psss. Another tender look at the rubies, which, after all, aren't rubies but how well they imitate rubies, how well they look like rubies, even if people criticize synthetic material, so what: the thing that matters is for them to look like it: her faith is in appearances, her religion is appearances, her motto of life is appearances: fate is a dance and anyone who doesn't put on appearances is a nance. Appearances, faking, and let's change the subject. Every Monday, every Wednesday, every Friday, the film of films, Bear of Berlin, Seashell of San Sebastián, Lion of Venice, Oscar of Hollywood, evening performance only, filmed in the place where the things happened, the things happen. Today, today, today: monumental opening of the monumental superspectacle in radiant sexocolor *Nipples Daubed with Honey.* Shots never shot. Forget the exhibitionist nonsense of Hedy Lamarr in *Ecstasy:* foolishness. Forget the buccal virtuosity of Linda Lovelace in *Deep Throat:* child's play. Forget the anal preference of Marlon Brando in *Last Tango in Paris:* old hat. Forget horizontal position nineteen: peepee people. Enter the twinkling curvature of our age, the multiple positionism of our age, the erotic pluralism of our age. Today, today, today: Old Man, conductor, play the clarinet solo for me. The Old Man, while she instrumentalizes the clarinet solo, a vocalist, with high notes: pleasure of gods, gods of pleasure. She, ill-mannered, talking away with her mouth full: but you. He interrupting her: when are you going to use the familiar form, the *tú,* with me, let's be familiar, the familiar form is the shortcut, the formal doesn't rhyme with *to* bed, *to* ask, or *to* demand the familiar because that's what I want *to* pay for, you *too?,* a monopoly of teeth, double-six in dominoes. The Old Man leaps like a little kangaroo. The Old Man is as graceful as an elephant. The

Old Man graceful as an elephant went after her in the supermarket because she was going around slacked up in a pair of
tight jeans. An Old Man went after her in the supermarket, the
man completely caught, the model of a man gone out of style,
out of date but with airs of a lady-killer. I'm going to beat The
Old Man and whoever wins can holler bingo: a resolution taken
when The Old Man followed her in and out through all the
shopping carts or shelves or display cases in the supermarket.
So resolute that it was going on six months since she'd hooked
up with The Old Man. The Old Man followed her and winked
at her, it's

A MATTER OF a few IOUs and the linoleum and the
little dining-room set I want in chrome: she sketches out minor
luxuries like a night table covered with an embroidered mat,
with lace trim. It isn't as if she's going to spend her whole life
with The Old Man, The Old Man makes her puke. But The
Old Man sends her the little green check of hope. Six months:
so much time being kept doesn't give her any piacere. The
advantage of being kept is that the eats are kept. The disadvantage of being kept is the obligation of getting up every morning
just the same: washing, ironing, cooking. That's why I admire
Iris Chacón: she talks about Iris Chacón the performer and she
gets an asthma attack. Because Iris Chacón isn't kept by anything except the danceable impulse of her body. At night she
dreams that Iris Chacón the performer, enwrapped in guarachile emanations, comes to get her: softlike, quietlike, secrety,
Iris Chacón the performer tells her. She never finds out what

Iris Chacón the performer wants to tell her because she wakes up, oh forget it no more IOUs and if I saw you I can't remember. Five o'clock and: so what difference does it make, her feet making a riot as if the belch were a green light for rollicking, the belch or Macho Camacho's ballocking guaracha *Life Is a Phenomenal Thing,* a guaracha that lights the stoves of people who aren't anywhere. Her breasts surge against the seams of her bra, rich and sinewy although doughy at the base. Her hips fall into a grind and her waist picks up the grind. Her head outlines one, two, three circles that correspond to the three gusts of joyful windiness that the trumpets expel; a ceremonial joy, a rite officiated in every corner of her body, a body elevated this afternoon to a temple of sweat with lively buttocks as ovalate and tremblish offerings. She remembered:

A FONDLING OF plastic grapes: they look so nice in a crystal bowl. No, she wasn't the only woman in slacks, although hers, brilliant white, stuck to her, were tight on her, with little, what can you say, little prudence. "Little decency," muttered one of the check-out women, protected by the solemn blouse designed by the wife of the American owner of this and many other supermarkets, a tight-twat Bostonian, prominent member of the Clean groups, a Mormon who was frightened and driven to seek out doctors and restorative salts because of Antillean sexual proclivities: dirty bunch that they are. She remembered, bring the right up over the left: legs. The Old Man ran his hands through his white hair with a gesture of studied indifference perfected in the intimacy of his double-mirrored wardrobe. With the same gesture of studied indifference, put on his dark glasses, unbuttoned his linen sport shirt so that a small poster of virility with a text of athletic chest could go on ahead, checked his appearance in one of the huge windows, and entered the supermarket in time to catch her turning the corner by the apples from Pennsylvania; she saw him first, peeping mom, keeping her eye on the masculinery as always, she didn't know whether to buy guava or orange or sweet-potato paste, which would go best with the white cheese: then and there, in the lapse of time spent in doubt, arrow-shot by the cheese itself, she came upon him as she faced one of the great dilemmas of her existence: whether to wed a sweet spread to Indulac cheese. Many years later, because it seemed like years to her as she faced the firing squad, because acceptance of the fact that The Old Man would possess her was nothing more than a firing squad, The Old Man told her that he told himself when he saw her: a chick is a chick is a chick, the cart loaded with elegant crackers, a small jar of elegant artichokes, several small cans of elegant smoked oysters, some elegant ham spread, elegant cider. Many years later, because it seemed like many as she faced the firing squad, and acceptance of the fact that The Old Man would possess her was nothing more than that, she told The Old Man that she told herself: nnnnnmmmmm. And she laid out a quick strategy of conquest: she waited for The Old Man to cross, cocksure cocky game-cock, in front of the refrigerated case with oranges from Florida in order to give an attention-getting shout: say, to a cashier, is Campbell's on sale?, more warlike the shout than Santiago and Close Spain, ancestral, shrill, villagy, Campbell's vegetable soup as a pennant of war. A popular explosion was yours, the sap and marrow of my land, a bugle call to my nubile heart, the gale of your kisses: The Old Man said weeks later.

She thought, for the thousandth time: this fucking man is talking Greek.

SHE WAITS BAREFOOT, fervent, she thinks that shoes impose a return to the street through some wandering instinct left over in each sole: learned in the Weekly Horoscope published in the press throughout the continent by Narciso Liquiñaco, Professor of Occult Sciences, an occultist who had discovered that fact through a study of the whinnying of young mares born under the sign of Scorpio. The Horoscopist lent his prestige to the notion that the will-o'-the-wisp of love enters through the soles of the feet: amatory subjects must take their shoes off in order to foster the divine event: she, hungering for mysteries, chasing the chances, wrote an extensive letter a page and a quarter long to the Grand Hierophant Walter Mercado in which she asked him to shed astral light on the curious fact concerning young mares and their whinnying. But the Grand Hierophant never answered her. Could the letter have been carried off by the tail of the comet that also carried off the old woman in her nightgown? Things there are that are never known: the mystery of the world is a world of mystery: a quotable quote. Correction: she, before discoveries and quick strategies, saw him get out of a big old car that made your hair stand on end. "My Mercedes," he said, his ears raised, car of cars: she thinks that she thought. Leaving time so the master of the car of cars could make an inspection to see if he had left enough space at both ends, leaving time so the master of the car of cars could cross over with a specific rhythm he said, with a highty mighty lighty little step she said, her mouth tried to find a small space in the monumental window of the monumental supermarket: for reasons of distance and class she should have been buying somewhere else but: knowing, growing, going places, she preferred towing her purchases from the supermarket where the richos with buckos in the banko laid in their supplies, she said what she thought: even if I spend two buckos on a cabo. She tried to find a little spot without the interruption of the ads for the week's specials: ham from Virginia, potatoes from Idaho, grapes from California, rice from Louisiana, meat from Chicago, apples from Pennsylvania, oranges from Florida. She sharpened her mouth, a stingy, hot little beak, quite stingy, a splendid belch came to her. But the effort was useless. "A person can't even see herself," she muttered, laboriously Chinesing her eyes, always Chinese, with a drive to find the edges of the broken pencil. With a gesture of uncontrollable rage, she closed her purse. Another act undertaken was to shit on the devil's mother. Another act undertaken was to push back a roller that was hanging down by her ear. The purse was black, rectangular, and white and had the advantage of going with slacks that were black, rectangular, and white.

THE PLASTIC FRUITS placed in a large bowl cheer up the table and a plastic tablecloth is bought that imitates lace and they take on the look of having to be touched because they seem to have just come off the tree, like the artificial flowers that when you touch them seem to be fresh-cut flowers from the garden. A little chrome set, a linoleum, a little chrome set or something more presentable, imitation mahogany, imitation cedar, imitation whatever: the important thing is for it to look like it and for it to be payable in easy installments: I've got three loans from three moneylenders and I asked Freckles Faíco for forty with fifty back: loans to buy the wigs at Finitas Fashion that seems to think it's a specialty shop in Condado. And forty to pay for the pants suit made for me by The Dove, a mute little fairy who sews divinely, without mentioning that you've got to keep his hand out of the spangle box. Maybe at Mendoza Furniture, buy at Mendoza Furniture where easy payments are something sure. Five o'clock and he hasn't come. I'll get out of debt and I'll tell him to. One more month and. She was thinking away, thinking away, she thinks away: I'll be an entertainer with the name of The Lobster Lady, and become famousss and give my opinionsss and sign autographsss; but I've got to improve my writing. I'd even start in a pissy little movie house where you've got to show your hair. Daring, ambitious, excessive, how much could Iris Chacón help me by laying out the steps of Macho Camacho's guaracha? If you turn around now, keeping your turn and your look quiet, you'll see her waiting seated: her look wandering: in order to pay for my star's clothing I'll have to lay some Navy jokers. Probably on Saturday. I wouldn't have to open my legs if Doña Chon had anything. But Doña Chon is as down-and-out as I am. The face of an absent person is what she has and a body of worry.

AND LADIES AND gentlemen, friends, if this Popular
Disco that's broadcast from Monday to Sunday, from twelve
noon to twelve midnight, by the number one radio station of
the Antillean quadrant had a boob-tube you would see a micro-
phoniatic sucked up by the goody-good sounds and the wild
taste that's made history.

A BOMB AT the University: a blast contributed by Muhammad Ali's right hand can't supply the overwhelming effect supplied by the news in the soul of. Jawbones that huddle in the antechamber of catatonia, goat-leaping eyes, seismic nose: the face senatorial. And the torso: a stampede, a herd of heartbeats, a dot on an EKG. Soliciting, urging, begging a thousand pardons for the previous interruption. Two thousand pardons won't do, won't pay the debt of the interruption, damn it, of the ecstasy of the moment, the ecstasy cuts the quadrant; an ecstasy that warns, an ecstasy that reminds that life is a phenomenal thing. A bomb at the University: all we needed. But they're all the same. Bela Lugosi, Frankenstein, The Creature from the Black Lagoon come out as beautiful people if they can stand the comparison with. Damned if they're not the same ones: the FUPI people, the FUPI people, the fupi, the fupi, the fu, the fu, the f, the f: he blows bubbles with the consonant like a congested baby. Indignant: but, but there's, but there's no, but there's no reason, but there's no reason to, but there's no reason to investigate: the sentence segmented by outpourings of rage. But there's no reason to be scared, but there's no reason to tiptoe through the ins and outs of a lawsuit, but there's no reason to allow the Commission on Civil Rights to damage and disfigure with their underhanded fight the noonday clarity of events. A wrath in allegro, a wrath molto appassionato, a wrath that gets his prick up: but I don't know how many times I've talked about the matter with the honorable members of the honorable Board of Education: in the hallways of the Banks they head, at cocktail parties given by the Industries they run, on the decks of the yachts they own, in the heavy idleness of the summer vacation islands of Saint John and Caneel Bay, at swims on the private beach at the Hilton, at banquets at the Cerromar; kick out the FUPI, drowned in a glass of Pommard white '45, kick out the FUPI, poisoned by Chivas Regal swallowed in one gulp, kick out the FUPI, boozed up on the treacherously cordial magic of a Grand Marnier, kick out the FUPI: eyes of a fried fish, snout of a hedgehog, rump of a rhinoceros: off with their heads. A chanson de geste: university gates opening to receive the Riot Squad, the National Guard: a fanfare of Anchors Aweigh My Boys, a fanfare of The Halls of Montezuma, a fanfare of Over Hill Over Dale. And if blood flows let it dry and be scrubbed clean. *El Mundo* is on our side, no need to ask about *El Nuevo Día*, Viglucci is on our side, A. W. Maldonado is on our side, the big guns are on our side.

WE BEG YOUR pardon, a thousand pardons, five thousand pardons won't pay the high price of another interruption but we interrupt to bring you the news that, according to the most opined opinion of the most impartialized impartial observers, the bomb of high destructive force that went off at the Faculty of Social Sciences of the University of Puerto Rico was not set by the usual political, agitator, extremist students since the bomb of high destructive force went off in the offices of the usual political, agitator, extremist professors. In fragments, in a scattering, in a constellation of pebbles: the effigies of

Betances and Hostos and De Diego, the bearded ones; the Puerto Rican flag shredded into red white and blue rags; the speeches of Albizu Campos singed and blackened. Extra note: the Dean of the Faculty of Social Sciences has asked for an investigation, the Chancellor of the University of Puerto Rico has asked for an investigation, the President of the University of Puerto Rico has asked for an investigation, the President of the Board of Higher Education of Puerto Rico has asked for an investigation, the President of the House of Representatives of Puerto Rico has asked for an investigation. Ladies and gentlemen, the bomb is being investigated. Friends, since it's a matter of a bomb and on and on and on, the investigation of the bomb won't take one year, the investigation of the bomb will take many years. Senator Vicente Reinosa—Vince is a prince and wise till his demise—leans his head on the steering wheel. The temporary defeat of his epic of blood deflates him. Round and round, like a defeated besieger, he gathers the cherished blood in buckets: from heads pounded by the liberty of truncheons, from faces mummified by the fraternity of truncheons, from backs bent by the equality of truncheons. Round and round, like an orchestra librarian, he picks up the score for chests that lead the fray: blood blisters, bruises, welts. Round and round, like an unhinged evangelist, he swallows the words essayed: because the order proclaimed by the ballot box, because the mirror of the law, because demostically speaking, because atheistic socialism, because the terrorism of ideas, because they shall not pass, because why the cause of

CAMPAIGN PROMISES: LET unnamed mangy buzzards and vultures vilify my final form as the man who speaks

to you today, Vinceisaprince, Vinceisaprince, Vinceisaprince:
rockets in unison launched by the Women's Committee for
Vince. If the man who speaks to you today does not attain
the peace we all desire at the University: the infamous finger,
the inflammatory finger: let us drive the moneychangers from
the temple: Muscovite minions, making up to Mao, fawning
on Fidel: exploding, the need for a glass of water, rever-
berated by the fierce applause and the comments that twinkle
in the heavens of their mouths: he's the one, there's nobody
can beat him, he's smart three times over, he sticks to the
truth like a piece of dough, he's the one, faces twisted like
figures in a grand guignol. A campaign promise: to bring to
our beloved land, to bring to the Puerto Rican hearth, to
bring to the Puerto Rican home, to bring to God's favored
country the dove of peace: Vinceisaprince, Vinceisaprince,
Vinceisaprince. A campaign promise: the liquidation once
and for all of nationalist, isolationist, and independentist
movements. The black woman up front all worked up: let's us
get us the fifty-first state, that's what being American is all
about: a ragamuffin hallelujah, with a raising of arms that
show support and round and round the Vinceisaprince, Vinceisaprince, Vinceisaprince. A campaign promise: what a big
joke it is on the men of this island, on the men of this country: the herd in stampede, an uproar in thoracic cavities:
down with the independentists, the black woman up front all
worked up dreams of George Wallace's arm and Betsy Ross.
The orator rounds it off: fooling the men of Puerto Rico
when at the opposite end stand universal men, citizens of the
globe, localism is simple-minded, limitation is stupid: Vinceisaprince, Vinceisaprince, Vinceisaprince. Borne out on shoulders, borne out on a river of cheers, borne out on the front
pages of the press of this country: buddy-buddy with Ché

Perón and King Faisal, fighting for the lead column with the fearsome murderer Tony the Bike: behold him here leaping over mountains, the future governor?: a speculative go on the part of an influential columnist who in the assignment of roles in the great theater of the world has taken on the role of Seer: a seer totemic in the pronouncement of his riddles: future governor?: a clipping clipped and pasted in a scrapbook and answered with a Parker pen and a broad ambition in a hand as firm as a slap in the face: yes.

YES, YES, YES: like a bridegroom who repeats his assent until it resembles hunger, a daytime dream of ruling, a nighttime dream of ruling, the ambition that corrodes him is an ulcer, an ambition cared for and changed like a diaper with the industry of a little ant, an ambition cultivated by acts of frothy gentility: a how is your little girl thrust through the fluttering heart of a stuttering new father: what a beautiful child, what fine features, the lass deserves a portrait painter from the seventeenth century; how many trips to the Ehret Funeral Parlor, how many trips to the Puerto Rico Memorial and the Buxeda Funeral Home, how many so sorrys given with a tormented face: this is a hard life that we suffer but relieved by the certainty that he will rest in peace, Samaritan that he was, and other grief-laden et ceteras; each handshake a computed vote, a pat on the back for an important idiot, dying to see you for a talented official, your uprightness is a beacon in the stormy sea of life for a judge who fills his tank with adulation and starts up divinely, an expert in pushing the button that stimulates that weakness, a surgeon of imperceptible flattery. Yes, yes, yes: permanently campaigning: put the mill out the window, ho, and see which way the wind will blow.

SENATOR VICENTE REINOSA—Vince is a prince with bright brains to evince—looks at the kingdom of heaven, then he makes versicles: the campaign has cost me one whole ball and half of the other: I worked hard to raise a little capital, wobbly little capital raised through a petitionary calvary: what honest politician hasn't gone through his Gethsemane: automobile raffles, hundred-dollar-a-plate dinners, telethons, the island premiere of that uplifting film *The Green Berets* with John Wayne's canonized bullets in the leading role: sighful is his good soul. My person cast aside, the only thing that doesn't matter, what matters is the accumulation of wishes: Women for the Re-election of Vicente Reinosa, Youth for Vince, Friends of Vicente Reinosa: waves of crusaders, waves of stickers put on waves of automobiles, waves of stickers with waves of mottoes, with waves of words alluding to my talent and good-fellowship: Vince is a prince and easy to convince, Vince is a prince with a conscience to evince, Vince is a prince and his goodness doesn't wince, Vince is a prince for the poor long since, Vince is a prince and his skill deserves a plinth, Vince is a prince and his ideas convince, Vince is a prince and as honest as chintz, Vince is a prince, no accidents, clean rinse, Vince is a prince and words doesn't mince, Vince is a prince and his word will convince, Vince is a prince and with honor ever since, Vince is a prince and his manner doesn't wince, Vince is a prince and marked to convince, Vince is a prince and his mind you can't rinse, Vince is a prince and respects dissidence, Vince is a prince and his guts never wince, Vince is a prince and pious as a quince, Vince is a prince and his honesty won't rinse, Vince is a prince and his calm makes you wince, Vince is a prince and wise till his demise, Vince is a prince with bright brains to evince: waves of propagandistic mottoes strung together by the admiration of an intelligence that admires mine. False, mottoes of his own sole invention and sole appreciation, even though he denied the authorship of the anonymous collection with a sanctimonious look and the flowered tunic of embarrassment and blushes.

IT'S GOOD THAT the schoolgirl, let's say her name is Lola, will get into the outside lane on the righthand strip, by which one supposes or is led to suppose that at the next traffic light she'll turn right. If Senator Vicente Reinosa—Vince is a prince and his pride doesn't wince—tails and trails the schoolgirl let's say her name is Lola, he'll go along through the harbor area, will observe the maritime maneuvers of the new invincible armada, will contaminate his soul burrow with pestilential grenades, will intersect the intersection of Bayamón-Cataño, will reach Punta Salinas on wings, he will enter through a sandy alley, in some cul-de-sac there'll be the car and the schoolgirl, let's say her name is Lola, like a roguish faun he will wait, he will wait to see her emerge like Venus from the foam, he will wait for the schoolgirl's thighs to slip away from him like frightened fish: it will be bad if being outdoors brings on a Lorcan flu, he'll cough the whole of the *Gypsy Ballads*. A Dantesque vision will consume him, a vision worthy of a Song by Maldoror, an imaginary life of Marcel Schwob, a new report by Brodie: the schoolgirl's wig, let's say her name is Lola, will hang from a grapevine, the teats of the burlesque *Mother of Eight* will hang from a cocoplum bush. Extraordinary, colossal, startling!: Lola isn't Lola, Lola isn't Lolo, Lola is Lole: a screaming queen, hormonic and depilated. Quick camera, movement adulterated by the rapidity that is acrobatical, chaplinical, tatical, totoical, cantinflical, woodyallenical, he'll run and he'll run and he'll run.

SO MACHO THAT it's frightening, looking on and on at the schoolgirl, aggressive is the chest he shoves forward so the belly will recede, looking on and on and on, forgetting about the deafening dissipation, forgetting about the delirium of dissipation, forgetting about the guaracha beat that fills the roadway with couples: the masses have got out of their cars, the masses have declared this Wednesday to be national guaracha day, the masses wiggle as they chorus *life is a phenomenal thing*. Official, the diagnosis is official: the guaracha plague has taken over the country from end to end: no one will escape the plague of Macho Camacho's guaracha. Official: Macho Camacho's guaracha is an epidemic. Looking on and on and on at his watch, considering on and on and on whether he has time to tail and trail the schoolgirl and get yet another catch for his insomniac animal. Senator Vicente Reinosa—Vince is a prince and his morale won't wince—after thinking it over and over.

AND LADIES AND gentlemen, friends, the most delicious and most sweet sound cuts through me the way it's going to cut through you, my feet get away from me, the joints in my torso get away from me, my sweat's all happy because Macho Camacho's guaracha has come to stay, live it up and dance Mama, live it up the way I do as I drop down and drop up.

THEY SPIT IN a thousand ways: Graciela Alcántara y López de Montefrío is unfamiliar with the catalogue of Puerto Rican spitting put together by a cuspidologist imported from Harvard University for the purpose of cataloguing Puerto Rican spitting: a clearing of the throat or an imperial working up of saliva that despoils the throat of its phlegm, the emission is noisy; spontaneous saliva that is spat out immediately, an emission in the middle registers; a thin saliva of watery content that is shot out between the teeth, a water-can emission. Graciela: rich and poor, man and woman, at all times, at the most unexpected moments, in the air-conditioned mall of the Plaza Las Américas she sees it, in the parasolled café of Las Nereidas she sees it: spitting, a déclassé custom of a déclassé country: Isabella and Ferdinand never should have. Her eyes examine with the dedication of flies the heroic Rodón that fills a wall: a girl or woman with a look of ancient and enigmatic sweetness, a girl or woman adorned with a large green bow: I'd like to fill some leftover spaces with things from here, backyard people are God's children too: democratic, well made-up, objective: something by that Homar, something by that Myrna Báez, something by that Martorell: but they're so tragic that if I put them in the dining room they'll take away the desire to eat, if I put them in the bedrooms they'll take away the desire to sleep, if I put them in the living room they'll take away the desire to talk. Of course there are always the hallways. But in the hallways I've hung the paintings we brought from Amalfi. Of course there's always the main foyer. But in the main foyer I've put the cases that hold my husband's coin collection. The heroic Rodón: girl or woman with hair blending into molasses. Fill the leftover spaces with scenes in Sèvres porcelain.

LIKE A DISTANT hello to our honeymoon in Guajataca. Like an homage to the eternalness of our love forged during the honeymoon in Guajataca. I explain when the upper crust went to Guajataca and the risk of not finding a seamstress or a model the same size was impossible. Like a distant hello, *that* is done on our anniversary or on a day when, for reasons of some festivity, my husband lets an excess of liquor bring on such an outrage: for some American senator the Resident Commissioner in Washington has asked us to entertain, some manufacturer from Georgia who wants to take advantage of our tax exemptions, some publicist from Wall Street: facts, snippets, hints, the intimate exposition intimidates her, she devours cigarettes. It intimidates her in spite of Doctor Severo Severino's vaselining of the session with a charm worthy of Madame Récamier's salon: the début of Alicia Alonso in the American Ballet Theatre, the nudes that Gabriel Suau never showed, Norman Mailer's scandals, the Tamayo that Rafi Rodríguez bought, the sculpture that Consuelo Crespi did, Visconti's scenery for La Scala, the writers on Fire Island, Judy Gordon's pretty people, the latest Buñuel, Borges' mother. It intimidates her in spite of the fact that Doctor Severo Severino lives his psychiatric profession with the sportiness of a pimp of neurosis, sewn and mended with spools of tolerance, greased with the butter of understanding. Doctor Severo Severino sees, discovers, catches a gesture, a twitch, a small attack of anger on the mouth of Graciela Alcántara y López de Montefrío when, from amidst the invisible mold of her hip-wiggle, there appears, zigzagging, Macho Camacho's guaracha: a guaracha that my servants have converted into a hymn, a street-corner hymn, a repulsive hymn, a hymn of the mob.

MONDAY, SHE MARKED Monday on the calendar because the Grand Hierophant Walter Mercado predicted family trouble for Virgos. Monday it was and she was in the desperate hope that noontime would strangle morning and afternoon would strangle noontime and night would strangle afternoon and night would close in over her fatigue, which wasn't fatigue but ennui and boredom. Monday it was and she rocked soul and sorrows in the Vienna chair, she was rocking her love affair with Chopin when Macho Camacho's guaracha *Life Is a Phenomenal Thing* burst into her house with the force of a river at floodtide. Violent, indignant, irritated, she called the servants by name, Chucha, Jacinta, and Josefa, and put Macho Camacho's guaracha *Life Is a Phenomenal Thing* into quarantine: a street-corner hymn, a repulsive hymn, a hymn of the mob. Choose: the guaracha or me. When her husband came home her husband was annoyed by what he considered hasty judgment, one lacking in the shallow study to which all value judgments must be submitted: I know all about that, as a member of thirty-three advisory committees of the legislature and twenty advisory committees of the executive. With the dramatic odor of leadership he reminded her that those street-corner people, that repulsive mob, had given him his seat in the

Senate. Because his area of electoral accumulation was made up of street-corner slums, repulsive mobs, the same ones she would have to visit as a civic duty of social uplift and neighborly love, accompanied by Pipo Grajales, Edi Crespo, or José García, photographers from the *San Juan Star*. Graciela wept. She wept like a Magdalene. She wept like a disconsolate child. She wept like a little orphan. Graciela said that the servants were more important than his wife of all those years. Graciela said that if her widowed mother were alive she would have moved out of that house. Graciela said that she hadn't been refined in Switzerland snowy and pure to return to the island and be treated shabbily. Graciela said how could he have thought like that. Graciela shut herself up in the matrimonial bedroom, locked the door, and wept like a Magdalene, wept like a disconsolate child, wept like a little orphan.

CHUCHA, COOK AND member of the street-corner gang, the repulsive mob, knocked on the door of the matrimonial bedroom: Doña Graciela, I don't want to bother you but the macaroni stuffed with raisins and cooked with mushroom sauce that's eaten with eggplant stuffed with plums in egg batter is getting cold. Amidst great tears, amidst a pulling of hair, Graciela answered: what do I care if the macaroni stuffed with raisins and cooked with mushroom sauce that's eaten with eggplant stuffed with plums in egg batter is getting cold: the vocal register at its highest. My husband slept on the couch after telling Chucha to do whatever she wanted to with the macaroni stuffed with raisins and cooked with mushroom sauce that's eaten with eggplant stuffed with plums in egg batter. The next morning the husband, crumpled, cramped, because the couch bends around a corner and can't hold a straight body, knocked at the door of the matrimonial bedroom: to ask you to forgive me, to ask permission to buy you two hundred dollars' worth of perfume.

GRACIELA CALLED ALICE and asked her if Vogue Souvenir was Jean Patou or Guerlain. Alice replied that she didn't know but that Jean Patou and Guerlain distilled so many distilled aromas, while Coco Chanel. But she didn't finish because I've got to hurry and get off the phone in a hurry because my little girl is going to make her début tomorrow in Villa Caparra and she's been crying like a little orphan because she hasn't got a date and the only date available is an ugly, terribly ugly boy with his face all broken out and he bites his nails. They call him Icky Ico and my Girl is scared to death that they'll christen her with the name of Icky Ica. And she hung up. Graciela called Susan, Susan called Maureen: Vogue Souvenir wasn't either Jean Patou or Guerlain or Coco Chanel: Maureen didn't know whose it was but she did know whose it wasn't. Graciela called Sheila's Mother. Sheila's Mother asked why not Caron's Bellodgia or Jean D'Albert's Écusson. Graciela called Joanne. Joanne suggested a box of Shalimar, a box of Chamade, a flacon of Narcisse Noir. Graciela went to the Perfumery at the Monte Mall and learned from the authoritative mouth of a Cuban perfumer that poor Marie Antoinette went to her date with Monsieur Guillotin steeped in fragrances by Houbigant: she was regal up to the very last in order to give a lesson in seductive hygiene to those smelly people Robespierre, Danton, and Marat: in Havana when I was going out to Country Club and it was rumored that Fulgencio was leaving, I put Shalimar on my legs, Narcisse Noir on my panties, Christmas in July on my bust, and Madame Rochas on my face.

PERFUMES TODAY AND the today divided up: perfumes today in the morning: dresses only yesterday: Marysol's boutique, Fernando Pena's winter collection, Rafaela Santos' marabou boa; jewels tomorrow: an opal set in the empty spot, a bracelet of tiger's-eyes, a pendant of lapis lazuli. Immediately following: a defeat of enthusiasms, the enthusiasm defeated by the permanent urge to do nothing: to stretch out on the bed, stretch out on her back, the ceremony of abandoning legs, the ceremony of abandoning arms, weightless dove, stretched out and reduced to a waist at rest. Doing nothing: returning to the bed through a chink that barely is a chink: a minimal opening, somnambulant, aware of the breadth of unhappiness, suckling unhappiness, singing a maxim to it: the grief of having been born a woman. She possesses the maxim as if it were a body. She smokes, smokes a second time, smokes many times. Doctor Severo Severino views the smoke, reviews the smoke, the disappearance of the smoke pushes his sensitivity to line up reflective asterisks about smoke: smoke is what we are, smoke is what we are, smoke is what we are: repeated, repeated. Had she tried to overcome her tedium vitae by joining civic clubs?: the look contracted by the traces of smoke. Graciela Alcántara y López de Montefrío strips down her smile: yes. And only recently she was a charter member of the Committee for the Design of Typical Puerto Rican Dress: she quit the Casa Club because her design had been rejected, a design that got away from typical dress with its dead weight of ruffles and beads. Because it was a high-fashion design: a tailored suit with a closed collar in spotted calfskin: a triumph of cosmopolitan taste over peasant le-lo-lai: down with gardenias, down with poppies, down with bell skirts. Mrs. Cuca White, Mrs. Pitusa Green, Mrs. Minga Brown, Mrs. Fela Florsheim, a topflight tetralogy of taste, recognized the advantages of a tailored suit with a closed collar in spotted calfskin, but, with regrets embellished with kisses, objected to the material used in its making: the sun here wreaks an impious vendetta, excessive perspiration might reinforce the thesis that our blood is mixed with leucocytes, erythrocytes, and platelets of intolerable Africanity. No, she didn't invent any reason or excuse to drop out, to storm out like a Scarlett O'Hara. But she left the Casa Club morally wounded: I cried like a Magdalene, I cried like a motherless child, I cried like a little orphan. Poor poor thing exclaimed with sorrowful sorrow by Doctor Severo Severino. Had she cultivated participation in and sponsorship of restorative activities like the annual concerts of the Casals Festival?: music moves us to the celestial spheres where the Goddess Purity dwells. Besides, the nights of the Casals Festivals are star-studded nights: who will ever forget the dazzling daring of Camile Carrión and her neckline plunging down to the lower lobes of her back in a lobby with reigning queens of equal bearing, a Cobián, a Valdés, a Rocafort?: enthusiast, enthused, enthusiastic.

CASALS FESTIVAL CULTIVATED, Trivia game cultivated, Botticelli game cultivated. Asking for Pablo Casals' autograph, Pablo Casals mansioned and slavered over by the governor of the moment: shouts of joy with the memory of Garbo's last picture, or Bergman's first picture for Rossellini, or the lead actor in the original *Blue Angel;* hearing the shriek of the other name for *The Lances* by Velázquez, hearing a question about *The Maids of Avignon,* hearing a question about the Duchamp in the Chicago Museum. Everything, everything, everything, crisis, crisis, crisis: a call from her husband: Dear, I'm going to be late, I'm drawing up the resolution in support of our glorious presence in Vietnam, she shrieked like a little rat with its tail in a trap: these walls are closing in on me, I moved to these hills to go insane, now I understand your satanic plan, enough of suburbs, I want to go back to Punta Las Marías, I want to go back to Garden Hills, I want to go back to the Paseo de Don Juan, we never use the swimming pool, we never give a pool party, we never use the terrace by the black orchid beds, we never use the big formal dining room, we never enjoy ourselves looking at your collection, we never eat on the tablecloths woven in Brussels, the Brussels tablecloths are rotting in their chests, we never go anywhere, when have we been written up in Judy Gordon's column, when has Judy Gordon said that we're *pretty people,* or that we're *very adorable people,* all I see is the face of the washerwoman, all I see is the face of the cook, all I see is the face of the gardener, all I see is the face of the maid, Pat and Raymond are in Europe and had an audience with the Pope, Lily and Ken are in Haiti and had an audience with Baby Doc: shouts, shouts, shouts. Her husband asked her to see a psychiatrist: I can recognize that the stress of modern life is building up this sediment of resentment. Honey, I don't blame you. The whole damn thing is your nerves. And here I am. I'm here. Like a ship adrift, like a ship that sets sail without any direction, like: and she fell silent. Silent, Graciela Alcántara y López de Montefrío is shaking the mauve suit designed by Ted Lapidus with nerves and other actions. Graciela Alcántara y López de Montefrío needs forty-five years—the forty-five years of her life, minute by minute—to reach this moment. Graciela Alcántara y López de Montefrío feels pure, explicit, invincible at the moment she asks: Doctor, do you like Macho Camacho's guaracha? Doctor Severo Severino lets his eyes wander around the bookshelves, lets his eyes climb up the spine of a small hedonistic manual entitled *Oh, the Milk Spilled for You.* Doctor Severo Severino, in the style of Rossano Brazzi, in the style of Raf Vallone, in the style of Omar Sharif, arches one eyebrow, arches the other eyebrow, begins to rub his thumbs together. Doctor Severo Severino, Maltese falcon, throws his head back, stroking his rough chin with his ring fingers. Doctor Severo Severino raises his left forefinger to a bottom molar. Doctor Severo Severino answers: when you come right down to it, yes. So,

AND LADIES AND gentlemen, friends, let me loosen the big boom, let me invite you to fasten your seat belts because we're about to take off, because it's one thing to call for the guaracha and another thing to see it come.

"NO MAN CAN ever give birth," said Doña Chon, bombastic in the formulation of the historic assertion, gratia plena. "Males, in spite of all and being males and being the ones in charge, are missing the important little screw in the push-ahead part that's an important little screw that a woman has from her start of having been born as a woman," said Doña Chon: gynecologist, ancient of the tribe. "The day a man wants to know what it's like to give birth, let him try shitting out a pumpkin," said The Mother: euphoric, a kindergarten in her ovaries, fanfare with the tubas of Fallopius. "Listen to this girl, you listen to me good this one time and let this one time be for all times," said Doña Chon, interrupted in her digression, kicked in her morality, offended in the beloved chastity of her ears. "Don't be so free with your words," said Doña Chon: a gesture transmitting why is this girl so free with her words. "It just comes out without my wanting it to," said The Mother, pouting, with the blameful face of what can I do it just comes out without my wanting it to. "Well, don't let it just come out without your wanting it to," said Doña Chon, intolerant, a hater of indecorous words. "Excuse me," said The Mother in her two-penny English. "When Tutú was born I was three days and three nights in labor," said Doña Chon, grandiose, the sweat of today pouring down with the memory of the sweat of yesterday, bombastic in the formulation of the historic assertion. "God have mercy," shouted The Mother,

dazzled by the historic assertion. "God have mercy," reshouted The Mother and the shout brought on a tight embrace that hurt them and they let go of each other. "Three days," reaffirmed Doña Chon, "three days and three nights that weren't two days and two nights or one day and one night": she folded the apron, put the apron into the only drawer in the chopping table, spoke with a tremulous ease: her emotions always shattered by the narration of hair-raising happenings: funerals, births that lasted three days and three nights, floods and knifings.

HIS EYES ARE wet, his gentle idiot peace broken, wet in order to narrow the cadence of the shadows that are building up a prison of shouts. His shoulders ready themselves to protect the gelatinous frame and move one toward the other. His eyes are wet. Trapped: in the dark net of his three ruinous and useless years. Trapped: by the anemic pity of the children who raffle off the jubilant opportunity to spit on him: me first I've got a cold, this one first he can hawk up snot.

"DOÑA PARTICULAR GARCÍA the midwife warned me, after inspecting my mother parts: Chon, resignation and pray what I tell you along with me: trouble is fine if it's one at a time. Chon, resignation to hear what I tell you: the child is coming out backwards and will go through this life backwards," said Doña Chon. Doña Chon was cutting the butcher's paper with which she wrapped up the fritters. Doña Chon sold four meat and plantain fritters to a flighty pregnant woman. Doña Chon scolded a flighty pregnant woman for not

being in bed. Doña Chon scolded a flighty pregnant woman for not being in bed and covered up from head to toe. "Right there I found out what the grief of being born a woman was," said Doña Chon, she exhaled with great force, which didn't blow out a candle because there wasn't any candle. "Chon, here's your husband so he can see you cry, Doña Particular García the midwife said," said Doña Chon. "Doña Particular García the midwife made the husband of the woman giving birth be present during the business of childbirth so he would learn and would really learn that calling the devil and seeing him come are two different things," said Doña Chon. "That not to pee and to pea a nut are two different things," said The Mother: she sketched out some steps, Macho Camacho's guaracha was escaping from the jukebox at the bar called The Sin of Being Alive. "Doña Particular García the midwife made five neighbor women be present in the house of the woman giving birth to help the woman giving birth push," said Doña Chon. "I remember deep in my memory that among the pushers who came to push came The Polacks," said Doña Chon. "The Polacks were called The Polacks because they were the daughters of Don Polo," said Doña Chon. "The Polacks pushed so much and so hard in the help they were giving me that one of The Polacks busted a blood vessel from so much pushing," said Doña Chon. "Great neighbors, The Polacks," said The Mother, in dancing deviltry because Macho Camacho's guaracha with its trumpeting blasts demanded dancing deviltry.

FROM THE HEART of the earth up to the sky there above, the same as from sleep to insomnia or hunger to food: any immense distance. From the far-off outlined in his eyes: a geography streaked with shadows. Far away, behind the far-off, from a thicket of shadows raised there, calmly stalking the lizard. The Kid: composed and taking refuge on an isle of drool. The Kid: calmly stalking the lizard. The lizard: dried, fried, crunched, hunched. The lizard: calculating and hypnotic stalking a chatterbox fly, a terse arabesque with the tail and a dangling threat. Lizard and chatterbox fly surprised in flagrante and swallowed in one mouthful, ingested, and acrobatics of the uvula and a torrent of saliva that rams and pushes. Three lizards a day and a pound of flies.

AND SHE WAS born backwards and she's going through life backwards: pained Doña Chon, unaccepting and sorrowful and accepting. "How many years did Tutú get?" asked The Mother, slowing down the rocking of the guaracha, like someone giving rhythm to mourning, abandoning the proper wiggle: a drum solo. Protesting, reprimanding, answering, Doña Chon, "I keep telling you every day, seven, and she's got six to go," kneading the back of Cuddles the cat, looking at The Kid's retching, invading the isle of drool, going along the alley, ignoring the jukebox brawl between the bars called The Sin of Being Poor and The Sin of Being Alive.

Which one is jukeboxing Macho Camacho's guaracha most? "Six years is no bargain," said The Mother, clapping and ass-setting, sweating fragmented eehs of guarachist devotion, chorusing the guaracha, throwing kisses to The Kid. "Six years is no bargain or swig of cane juice," said Doña Chon, dusting off the Prayer to Saint John of the Conquest, dusting off the Prayer to the Holy Shroud, dusting off the Prayer to the Angel of Those Without Angels, making the sign of the cross over a battalion of flies that were quenching their thirst on The Kid's mouth. "They hand out a lot now to people who push stuff," said The Mother: the shake of a newly bathed dog, the shake of a setting hen, a most shaky shake. Kissing a Crucifix, kissing a Sacred Heart of Jesus, kissing a Palm from Palm Sunday, Doña Chon said, "For the rich they look the other way. The rich selling grass under the government's nose, offering stuff to everybody and his cousin." "Connecting with dope, connecting with good grass," said The Mother, "connecting with Macho Camacho." "For poor people, seven years in the dark," said Doña Chon: grimacing, resenting, hating. "Doña Chon," said The Mother, dropping her body to the ground, beating the ground with her shoulders, dancing, "if you take The Kid for me this afternoon I'll give you some dough at night and that dough and a little more will help pay Tutú's lawyer. They land on a two-bit pothead, but potheads in Villa Caparra and Garden Hills are happy as larks." Doña Chon says, "If I have to pick up The Kid, I'll pick up The Kid, let it all be for Tutú, although if it wasn't for . . ."

FRECKLEFACE, GIVEN THE job of sponsoring the adventure in friendship, ties him with a little cord, pulls on him, feeling lord and master, his smile arrogant. When the others arrive, like a flock of pigeons, Freckleface is strutting, Freckleface is vainglorious: they gave me The Booby. The surprise spreads out like a frothy champagne, like frothy beer. The surprise is raised on high up to the clouds, surprise of everyone. Everyone, not one was left out, hurried, rushed, avalanched: to ask the loan of him, to beg the loan of him, to beseech the loan of him, leaping like happy dogs, like panting dogs, envy in bloom, evil in bloom, loaned to be a pony, loaned to be a rocking horse, loaned to be a bear, loaned to be a bridge, loaned to be a swing, loaned to be a seesaw, loaned to be a stool to sit on, loans granted willingly. The acacias, the acacias rocking, the acacias delicate, the acacias incapable. "Lend him to me," shouts one, a shout with shit for a surname, holding a piece of mirror, a mirror gripped as a weapon, a mirror from which the reflections sprouted, a mirror that's flooded with faces, faces that enter and exit from the piece of mirror, a mirror where a prophecy crouches.

"ALTHOUGH IF IT wasn't for Tutú, if it wasn't for the debt owed Tutú's lawyer, if it wasn't for this bundle of dirty clothes that life is," said Doña Chon, "I wouldn't help you by picking up the little one, you could take that song somewhere else: sun baths." Heated. Denying. Disbelieving. "The sun like an onion will beg your pardon and do its best to give you a hard-on," said The Mother, she was folding back her shoulders into an amusing fan, she was opening and closing her shoulders so that her breasts leaped and jumped in fun. "I need the bucks, the bucks, the bucks," said The Mother, said with an oath, said with an oath by that Father Which Art In Heaven, said ringing bells, said dancing Macho Camacho's guaracha: to two rhythms, to two beats, to two records: a record in the bar called The Sin of Being Poor, a record in the bar called The Sin of Being Alive. "A monkey dances for dough," said Doña Chon, looking at her twist, looking at her falling apart, looking at her contorting, looking at her rubbing herself, looking at her flying off. The Mother said, "Doña Chon, what do you mean?"

she said twisted, said fallen apart, said contorted, said rubbed, said flown off.

A HANDFUL OF hands, a handful of wills, scrambling, a riot of fingers, the mirror elevated like a chalice, the piece of mirror elevated like a sacred host. Until The Kid's face poured into the piece of mirror, uncontained. The great head raised, held erect, sustained by ten hands. The Kid, waking to the horror of his own horror, tears a protesting whine wrapped in weeping from his throat. Then, all the pain of the world skewers him in the heart and the sky turns dull like an unwashed wooden floor: seamy and mean. A bird that beats its spurs, a broken siege, the flight will never end, the deboned arms, the arms thrown back: toward the freedom of the drool: without planning, without thinking: planned by horror and ugliness. Running is pleasing and free, he discovers it without discovering it, running, disappearing like a dot, unreachable by the shouts that shout at five o'clock in the afternoon, Wednesday afternoon today.

AND LADIES AND gentlemen, friends, here is the guaracha by the Tarzan of culture, the Superman of culture, the James Bond of culture, here is and we have here Macho Camacho's ecumenical guaracha *Life Is a Phenomenal Thing.*

NO SOONER HAD Bonny climbed onto the hambone-thick thighs and one foot dropped anchor at the stern of the ship sinking between two waves: the tattoo, no sooner had Bonny let his cold and indifferent lips alight on the feigning and demanding mouth of La Metafísica, no sooner had Bonny given the hint of some tense ass-twitching, than Benny burst into the loading and unloading zone or room of La Metafísica and shouted a terrorist command of *dismount* that made Bonny alter and falter. Bonny, altered and faltered, got out of the way with a kangaroo leap, safe and seated on La Metafísica's navel: recounted days later amidst so much laughter that it made them squint: into La Metafísica's well of sin they stuck a sparkler that turned La Metafísica into an enlightened whore. La Metafísica, a Japanese wrestler, couldn't wrestle or joust, her working tool singed. La Metafísica kicked, raged, cursed, said she would take her case to court: the friend of adjudicators, official devirginizer of reigning officialdom, trained in the workshops of Isabel La Negra, improved in the brothels of Carmen the Rooster and Jenny Crablice, leading lady at the prestigious fucking place Educative Traits. La Metafísica let toads and snakes fill her mouth and asked for water: water, it's burning my, curious that she never named the unnamable: superstitious. After three days, without having recovered, she demanded justice and indemnification, she went hither and yon, she thundered, she rolled through all the

205

branches of Social Security, she petitioned the Workers' Accident Compensation Authority for a pension, she brought a complaint to the Department of Consumer Services. No use: La Metafísica was unheard at bureaucratic unhearings: there's no case, the case is of a lesser degree, when the case reaches its turn for consideration the effects of the attack will have disappeared. In sum, the occupational hazards of her trade, although she swore: sooner or later they'll hear from me.

BENNY, BONNY, WILLY, and Billy, in the future, in order to avoid unpleasantness, in order to avoid storms, in order to wait for the high tide of mistrust to recede: the counsel of the council of fathers brought together to examine, with adult gravity, the gravity of the matter: a meeting held in the right wing of Benny's Mami's molto bello gardeno, white wicker chairs, the uncorking of six bottles of Dom Perignon and the passing of little polished silver trays on which the smoked oysters and little rolls of octopus marinated in wine reposed. The lads should be separated, the lads should take a break for a few months from the riot of their beautiful friendship: jokes like that take place in the joking environment of every age: I cannot deny that I regret the sudden death of a sense of humor, you, humor, who more than humor are the spice of life: the elevated words of Papi Papikins, Baccarat glass elevated, his face elevated in the quest of ideas that are noble and elevated.

BENNY CONFESSES TO the Ferrari: you're the only one who understands me, only you and me: but he doesn't finish. Benny adds himself to a protest that takes the form of a claxonic cloud at five o'clock sharp in the afternoon. Benny, bored with trotting back and forth from San Juan to Caguas and from Caguas to San Juan, trotted that afternoon to Isla Verde Beach, to Boca de Cangrejos. The highway free of heavy traffic let him make sixty-mile-an-hour tracks although he had to brake fast so as not to end up in the sands of Piñones. In the end: returning after to this miserable tie-up, going through Villa Palmeras, going down Morell Campos, getting onto the Avenida Borinquen, and taking a shortcut through the Cantera slums. Shortcut no way, the tie-up was the same, trapped in one of those side streets where the Goddess Mita has her emporium of faith: grocery stores, furniture stores, money stores, restaurants. Annoyed, Benny doesn't look at the look of the two girls looking at him from the Toyota, girls who look at him and laugh, look at him and flirt. Curious, because Benny had desisted from girls when he began to put together his exceptional photothèque with covers torn from *Playboy, Oui, Penthouse, Screw,* covers with which he shared his urgencies, a poster of Sophia Loren with her nipples made transparent by the rain, a poster of Raquel Welch with her two plaits of hair as her only attire, a poster of Ivonne Coll with a dress that proclaimed the softness of her breasts. Then the Ferrari arrived and the rest is well known. Before the Ferrari and the photothèque came the dates with Sheila. L'affaire Sheila gelded him for a time, gelded with six letters, a time in which he wasn't even content with his hand, gelded by Sheila or, to do proper justice: gelded by Sheila's Mama.

WELL, THE FACT is that Sheila, lyrical, refined, pearly white, didn't make a pass or leave an opening. Curious, because Sheila's Mama did make passes and did leave openings. Sheila's

Mama made passes and left openings with the discreet charm of the bourgeoisie, but everything ended up being known: it was known, or everybody came to think they knew that Sheila's Mama was a nymphomaniac and that on the walls of the membranous and fibrous conduit that in female mammals extends from the vulva to the matrix she had a trap called a siphon which was of the greatest danger for any male. Benny wasn't aware of the siphon. Benny became aware during the only occasion on which he fornicated with Sheila's Mama that Sheila's Mama was expansive in the bedroom and permitted herself unnecessary cackling: no way, that in the penetration Sheila's Mama had a laughing attack that changed into a weeping attack. What begins badly ends badly: Benny arrived at the wrong time to pick up Sheila, in the middle of the afternoon. Sheila wasn't home: Sheila's at the library Sheila's Mama informed him, dressed in a peignoir with promissory gauzes and underneath, of course, bra and panties: Sheila's Mama isn't a slut in Carmen the Invincible's casa di toleranza nor did she pass her formative internship in a cabaret where all manner of flashy trash has its abode. No. Sheila's Mama is a domestic smuggler. Domestic and with a deathly secrecy because Sheila's Papa is a cuckold with a whole string of yea-hoos of the kind that could chop anybody's life in two. The day Sheila's Papa finds out that Sheila's Mama is cheating on him he's going to have an attack of the Mexican charro syndrome and Sheila's Mama and whoever is rooting around with her are going to end up with more holes in them than a square yard of wire mesh. Sheila's at the library Sheila's Mama said and Sheila's Mama let a breath of air enliven her peignoir: Benny stammered thanks when Sheila's Mama served him a glass of beer and invited him up to the bedroom: in the bedroom, with the seduction worthy of one of Pharaoh's courtesans, Sheila's Mama undressed Benny without asking his permission, the peignoir rested on a reclining chair. Benny wanted to go by coming: but Sheila's Mama was an adept of conversatory coitus and Socratic dialogue: dialogue and a laughing attack and a weeping attack and possess me and don't possess me and possess me so I feel possessed and swear to me that even though a long time passes you won't forget the moment I knew you and shouts in the hallway and shouts on the stairs and the furious shouts of Sheila's Papa who arrived without warning and Sheila's Mama invented a migraine, a prostration, a let me have some peace for once in your life: Benny collapsed in the closet, collapsed in the closet waiting for the shot. Gelded for a good while.

FINALLY, I MEAN finally I scrub the main road and take a little slice of this street and I surprise the blah-blah of those women and I shovel it all the way down the Calle París and I see that the Ferrari is smiling with happiness, I brake and turn fast down that street and I eat up that well-eaten straight line and I fall into sixty: hey Ferrari don't quit now: what rich madness, what mad richness. Falling into sixty and getting up to seventy: Ferrari big daddy. Ferrari big stud. Ferrari big macho: in a delirium. And tailing after the delirium the tail of the guaracha: a serpent that lashes with its savor, Benny lashed with savor. Greeting eighty through the narrow streets until. It wasn't my fault to some women who scream in horror. It wasn't my fault to some children who turn the corner. It wasn't my fault to an old woman who has an attack and crosses herself and says I got held up paying the lawyer. It wasn't my fault to some brains splattered on the door of the Ferrari and to some eyes plopped in the gutter like the yolks of half-fried eggs.

Benny doesn't hear frights. Benny doesn't hear laments. Benny doesn't feel the afternoon breathing with difficulty. Benny doesn't see dusk commence its guerrilla attack against the empire of blues. Benny asks, rusty, hurried by his hurry: I mean when will I be able to wash my Ferrari?: the voice shrill and rancor hurting him: I shit on God's grandmother.

Full text of Macho Camacho's guaracha

LIFE IS A PHENOMENAL THING

Life is a phenomenal thing,
frontwards or backwards, however you swing.
But life is also a groovy street,
it's coffee for breakfast and bread that you eat.
Oh, yes, life is a nice chubby chick
spoiling herself in a Cadillac trick.
The trumpet breaking up the ball,
don't let the maracas back down,
the drums heard way across town,
the thing can't have any stop,
black women want sweat to mop,
black women are getting hot.

Green Village Condominium, Río Piedras, Puerto Rico
Hotel Luxor, Copacabana Beach, Rio de Janeiro

DISTINGUISHED LATIN AMERICAN FICTION FROM BARD

By Jorge Amado

DONA FLOR AND HER TWO HUSBANDS	54031	$3.95
GABRIELLA, CLOVE AND CINNAMON	51839	$3.95
HOME IS THE SAILOR	45187	$2.75
SHEPHERDS OF THE NIGHT	39990	$2.95
TENT OF MIRACLES	54916	$3.95
TEREZA BATISTA: HOME FROM THE WARS	34645	$2.95
TIETA	50815	$4.95
TWO DEATHS OF QUINCAS WATERYELL	50047	$2.50
VIOLENT LAND	47696	$2.75

By Gabriel Garcia Marquez

AUTUMN OF THE PATRIARCH	51300	$2.95
IN EVIL HOUR	52167	$2.75
ONE HUNDRED YEARS OF SOLITUDE	45278	$2.95

BETRAYED BY RITA HAYWORTH Manuel Puig	36020	$2.25
DOM CASMURRO Machado de Assis	49668	$2.95
EMPEROR OF THE AMAZON Marcio Souza	76240	$2.75
EPITAPH OF A SMALL WINNER Machado de Assis	33878	$2.25
THE EYE OF THE HEART: SHORT STORIES FROM LATIN AMERICA Barbara Howes, Ed.	54346	$3.95
THE GREEN HOUSE Mario Vargas Llosa	42747	$2.25
HOPSCOTCH Julio Cortazar	53991	$3.95
THE LOST STEPS Alejo Carpentier	46177	$2.50
SEVEN SERPENTS AND SEVEN MOONS Demetrio Aguilera-Malta	54767	$3.50

Available wherever paperbacks are sold, or directly from the publisher. Include 50¢ per copy for postage and handling: allow 6–8 weeks for delivery. Avon Books, Mail Order Dept., 224 West 57th St., N.Y., N.Y. 10019.

(Lat Am 6-81) (1-1)

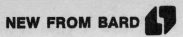

NEW FROM BARD

DISTINGUISHED MODERN FICTION

TALES OF PIRX THE PILOT
Stanislaw Lem   55665 • $2.95

Here are five comic adventures of a bumbling space
cadet by the author of THE CYBERIAD, and "one of
the most intelligent, erudite, and comic writers today."
Anthony Burgess, *The Observer* "These stories are
clever and alive—pure gold." *Boston Globe*

THE RIO LOJA RINGMASTER
Lamar Herrin   55673 • $3.50

This is the award-winning novel of Dick Dixon, a base-
ball player looking for the perfect victory in his game,
his life, and his love. "Vitality, humor, intelligence and
vividness." *Washington Post*

ELEPHANT BANGS TRAIN
William Kotzwinkle   56549 • $2.75

"The 16 pieces herein are like the random shots from
a Roman candle; all with a special brilliance; no two
alike in color, shape, direction, or tangent. . . . What
(Kotzwinkle) really is is a heckuva writer, with a wildly
imaginative wit and wisdom; clever and capricious as
a vagrant wind at a hemline; disciplined as a Marine
Corps D.I. in attention to detailed specks of explosive
grit." *Boston Globe*

THE WEATHER IN AFRICA
Martha Gellhorn   55855 • $3.50

Distinguished novelist and journalist Martha Gellhorn
unveils deep, personal sides of the precariously balanced black and white societies of East Africa. "Skillful
evocations of Africa's magnificent vistas and mysterious rhythms. . . . A work of total integrity and genuine
distinction." *Baltimore Sun*

Available wherever paperbacks are sold, or directly from the
publisher. Include 50¢ per copy for postage and handling;
allow 6-8 weeks for delivery. Avon Books, Mail Order Dept.,
224 West 57th St., N.Y., N.Y., 10019.

AVON Paperbacks

Bard (6) (10-81)